# BELLAMY

## THE CAMBOY NETWORK
### BOOK 2

## LINDEN BELL

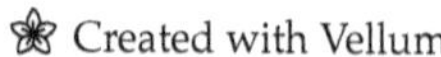 Created with Vellum

# BELLAMY

# BELLAMY

**There's a thin line between love and hate.**

## BELLAMY

I don't know how we ended up as rivals, but I couldn't have asked for a better nemesis than Noel. It's fun throwing insults and watching him lose his shit in public. He's cute when he's angry.

The world thinks he's a grumpy bad boy, but I'm not sold. The more I get to know him, the more I'm convinced there's a squishy marshmallow center underneath his hard shell.

## NOEL

Golden boy Bellamy drives me up the freaking wall. All I want to do is wipe that smug, arrogant grin off his face-- not necessarily with my hand.

I hate him, but the truth is I can't keep my hands off him. Our rivalry has always been explosive, and it turns out, so are we.

*Bellamy is an enemies-to-lovers, grumpy/sunshine, opposites attract MM romance between two camboys, each vying for the* *top spot. Expect secret hotel rendezvous, hate f*cking, and oiled-up wrestling. It is the second book in The Camboy Network series and can be read as a stand-alone.*

# CONTENTS

# PROLOGUE

## NOEL

Cameras love me. It's not bragging if it's true.

I pan my gaze across the bank of photographers, all of them shouting my name, eager for me to grace them with a fevered glance, a seductive quirk of lips. The bright floodlights dotting the red carpet are hot, turning the early evening chill into a midday summer heat. I'm cool though, calm and collected, as I pose with my shoulders back and chin up. The only thing heated about me is the smolder etched firmly on my face.

This isn't the first time I've walked a red carpet—rich parents come with perks—but it is my first time in this new persona I've created for myself. Edgy bad boy. Dark and brooding. Cocky and arrogant as fuck. The media loves it as much as the fans do and it's kind of freeing getting to be the asshole who doesn't care about anything or anyone.

"M-Mr. Carrington?" An event staff for the Grabby Awards tiptoes up to me with eyes as wide as saucers. "Hi, um…" He swallows visibly and takes a breath like he's working up the courage to keep speaking. "You can move to the interviews now," he says, voice breathy with an air of reverence.

I offer him a sly curl of a smile. "Thanks."

His cheeks flush and he catches his bottom lip between his teeth. His eyes are unblinking as he watches me walk past him. It's so amusing when fans stroke out from such a minuscule bit of attention.

He points me toward the row of interviewers, each holding an oversized foam-covered microphone that they shove unceremoniously in my face while firing off the same set of questions again and again.

"What's it like being nominated for one of the most prestigious awards in the adult entertainment industry?"

"What do you think of the other nominees in the Best Newcomer category?"

"Who do you think will win?"

*Who will win?* I lean over the barrier separating us and pin the interviewer with a teasing, unapologetic smirk. "Me," I rumble directly into the mic.

The interviewer's grin widens and his gaze drops to my mouth. "In that case," he meets my gaze with a knowing look, "I wish you the best of luck."

"Noel!"

I flash the camera one more sultry glance before turning away.

Sebastian Silver is waving at me from the end of the red carpet. "Melting the underwear off the interviewers?" he asks as I approach.

I shrug even as my lips twitch with a smile. "Something like that."

"It wouldn't be hard, with that outfit." He scans me with an appraising eye and my inner peacock preens at the compliment.

I've gone for a Karl Lagerfeld look, sourced directly from the man himself—tight leather pants, oversized black tie, black suit jacket, and lacy fishnet gloves. I've left off Karl's signature high-collared white shirt and opted for a bare chest instead. It is a porn awards show after all. Some skin is mandatory.

"Have you scoped out your competition yet?" Sebastian asks when we're ushered into the hotel ballroom.

"Some."

Lies. The first thing I did when the nominees were announced was look up the four other guys in my category. Three of them are meh, forgettable, generically good-looking, and easily mistaken for each other. The last one though... Bellamy Blais is in a class all his own.

The first time I watched his video, I got that feeling in the pit of my stomach. The one where envy and jealousy, annoyance and attraction all swirl together in a sour mix. I wanted to hate the video, to hate him, but I couldn't tear my eyes away from the image of him on the screen.

Trying to describe Bellamy Blais is misleading. Half the guys in the room have the same dirty blond hair and clear blue eyes. But there's nothing common about the soulful way he stares into a camera. How he smiles like he and the viewer are the only two people in on the joke. The shapely curve of his plump lower lip.

Bellamy Blais is my only real competition.

"There he is." Sebastian nods toward the other side of the ballroom where Bellamy's standing with a bunch of surfer dudes. Tanned skin, sun-kissed hair, blinding-white teeth that he shows off with that mile-wide grin. He and his bros are wearing those fake tuxedo collars and cuffs that make them look like strippers at a bachelorette party. The sparkly short shorts do nothing but accentuate his dick print.

I get that feeling again. It makes me want to march over there and… it's a toss-up between shoving him and kissing him. Maybe both.

"Rumor mill says it's either him or you."

Bellamy lifts his head and turns in our direction. For a second, I think he's spotted me, that he's sizing me up the way I'm sizing him up. But then his gaze slides right past without a flicker of recognition, not even a fraction of a pause.

Resentment claws at me. I want to be the one standing on stage tonight. I want him to look up at me and feel this thing I feel. He's not better than me. He's not anything special. It's going to happen. I can taste the victory already.

Sebastian and I take our seats as the house lights dim and the show starts. It's filled with snicker-worthy innuendos and smutty jokes. It drags on and on and as much as I try to pay attention, my gaze keeps drifting back to the golden boy sitting on the other side of the room.

When it's finally our turn—*my* turn—I'm so twisted up inside that my smolder feels more like a glower. I *have* to win this thing. I *need* it.

"And the winner for Best Newcomer goes to…"

I hold my breath, willing my name to come out of the presenter's mouth. Every muscle in my body is taut in anticipation. It's going to be me. It has to be me.

"Bellamy Blais!"

The table across the room explodes in screams before my brain has even processed those four syllables. Sebastian pats me on the arm with a sympathetic look, but other than that, it's like I don't exist anymore. I'm nothing. I'm nobody.

All eyes are on Bellamy Blais, where his dude bros have hoisted him up on their shoulders. They carry him all the way to the stage while he laughs, loud and boisterous and carefree. Standing under the spotlights, holding that statue in the air, he looks like the fucking sun is shining down on him.

My stomach clenches almost painfully and my fingers itch to snatch the award out of his hand. That thing is supposed to be *mine*. *I'm* the one who should be standing up there—*I'm* the one who's special. How dare he think he's better than me? How dare they pick him over me?

"Hey, you okay?" Sebastian leans over after Bellamy finishes rambling through his acceptance speech and is escorted off the stage.

"Yeah, I'm fine," I say through gritted teeth and a pasted-on smile. I am fine. Or I will be. The fuckers around me don't know what they're doing anyway—giving the award to Bellamy. They're so shallow, they wouldn't recognize real talent if it pried open their jaws and fucked them in their mouths. I'm better than all of them. I don't need them.

By the time the show ends, I'm ready to get the hell out of there. There are half a dozen afterparties I'm supposed to go to—networking and all that—but they don't deserve to have me grace them with my presence. They don't think I'm good enough to win the damn award? Fine. Then I'm not good enough to go to their damn parties either.

Except I do go. Because fuck them, I'm going to order all of their best alcohol and drink them dry. And also because Sebastian latches onto my arm and doesn't give me any other choice.

The second we arrive, Sebastian is off, networking his little heart out. I'm too bitter to do anything but lounge in our VIP booth with my glass tumbler and a bottle of top-shelf whiskey.

No sooner am I settled, than in walks Mr. Golden Boy himself. The club goes fucking wild. I can't actually see him through the crowd of admirers who have mobbed him. But I can track his progress across the dance floor by the mass of bodies that undulate around him like some sort of amoeba wriggling its way forward. It's only when he gets to his own VIP booth on the other side of the club that the crush clears enough for me to see him.

He's still wearing those sparkly short shorts, but he's taken off the collar and cuffs. The multi-colored lights paint his skin like he's some sort of moving modern art. The line of well-wishers wind around the club, and he smiles at every person who comes up to say hello. Meanwhile, I haven't had a single visitor.

I toss back the whiskey in my glass and pour myself another. The liquor warms a trail down the middle of my chest and pools in my stomach. It's fuel to the sour churn of ugly feelings that have taken up residence there. Envy, jealousy, anger, hate. I want to ball it all up and shove it in Bellamy's face. I want to wipe away his smile with it, then cram it down his throat.

I drain my glass again and slam it down on the table in front of me. I need to get the fuck out of here. I can't sit and watch everyone who's anyone in the industry fawn over how good and perfect he is.

There's no way he's so good and perfect, though. No one is—not like that. Underneath all those bright and cheery smiles has to be a selfish, calculating mind. How else could he fool everyone into loving him when there's nothing special about him to love? He's a fake. He's a fraud. And I'm going to do everything in my power to make sure the whole freaking world knows it.

He doesn't realize it yet, but Bellamy Blais has just made an enemy out of me.

# CHAPTER
# ONE

## NOEL

"Oh my god, my cheeks hurt," Rhys pokes himself with two fingers on either side of his face and wiggles them in circles. "Who knew smiling was so much work?"

"I could've told you that," I say, cocking an arrogant eyebrow. One benefit of being a brooding bad boy is I never need to smile, so I'm never in danger of having sore cheeks—at least, not those kinds of cheeks. Heh, I'm hilarious.

Rhys shoots me a long-suffering glare. "Shut up. Not all of us can be grumpy assholes," he says before breaking out into another mega-watt smile for the fans approaching our booth.

The Camboy Network is the porn production company that Sebastian set up recently. It's a cooperative or collective or commune of some kind where we're all supposed to pool our camboy resources to reach for the stars. Or something like that. Rhys and I and our other friend Hayden all got recruited as founding members—as if we ever stood a chance against Sebastian's force of nature. I might've been skeptical at first, but even a grumpy asshole can be won over sometimes.

We're doing well—really well. Which is why when Sebastian floated the idea of signing up for a booth at the country's largest porn convention, I offered to foot the astronomical bill. What I didn't offer was to man the booth during the convention, but apparently, I'm a sucker for Sebastian's puppy dog eyes routine.

"Holy shit, you're Noel Carrington!"

I turn my practiced bad boy smirk onto two women who are clutching each other in their excitement. "That's me."

They've got bras for me to sign. They're not the first. I've scribbled on more bras and women's panties than I can count since I became a gay porn star. You have to appreciate the irony. But then, I've also signed my fair share of jockstraps and boxer briefs. After I've smoldered into their camera phones and they've bounced off, shrieking, Rhys taps me on the elbow.

"Look, your favorite person." He nods toward the giant screen hoisted high above the convention hall floor.

I don't need to look to know who Rhys is referring to. I've only got one "favorite person" and his face is currently plastered on every single wall in this damn hotel. Everywhere I turn, there he is with his too-bright smile, taunting me, mocking me, and that old familiar hatred eats away at my insides.

Bellamy fucking Blais.

It's been five years since I lost out to him at the Grabby Awards and my abiding resentment toward him is still holding strong. Everyone knows how I feel about him—

and when I say everyone, I mean everyone. Noel Carrington versus Bellamy Blais is the most talked about subject in the porn industry. It's a rivalry for the ages; it's legendary. I never pass on an opportunity to badmouth him in public and Bellamy's not shy about returning the favor.

If our feud converts more fans and paying subscribers to my cause—and it does—then that's a convenient side effect. But even if it didn't, I'd still cut him every chance I get.

He's seated between two beefcakes for a panel session in some other part of the hotel, wearing a plain white tank top thin enough for his nipples to show through. Closed captions scroll across the screen so I can't miss a single word he says.

*He was delighted at the invitation to visit the famous kink dungeon for his latest video. He had a great time getting tied up and edged by two very skilled and experienced doms. Yes, he would definitely do it again.*

*Would you like to see Noel Carrington get edged?* An interviewer's question pops up on the screen.

I fold my arms across my chest and glower. I'm not surprised they've dragged me into it. I'd be shocked if they didn't. The media is always looking to stir up shit between us. Pit Noel and Bellamy against each other and watch the sparks fly. It's good for the ratings.

Bellamy chuckles and shakes his head like that's the most amusing thing he's heard in ages.

"Uh, maybe you shouldn't watch this." Rhys tugs on my arm.

If there was a way to avoid seeing Bellamy's smug face every-fucking-where, I would have done it already. As it is, I'm better off knowing exactly what he says when he says it than waiting to hear about it over social media.

Still, I brace myself, my stomach churning with too much bile the way it always does when I think about the fucking fuckface.

*Noel Carrington?* He winces in disgust and the expression feels like a cheese grater across my skin. *I don't know, man, I don't think he'd last very long.*

The rest of the panel titters beside him as I clench my jaw to keep from shouting profanities at the screen. Around me, people sneak not-so-discreet glances in my direction, snickering, waiting for me to put on a show for them.

"Goddamn motherfucker." I don't quite shout it, but I definitely don't bother keeping my voice down. The whispers around me grow louder.

Rhys looks concerned. "You want to take a break? Go out and get some fresh air?"

I shake my head, feet planted right where they are, eyes glaring missiles at the screen. "I'll wait for Sebastian and Hayden to get back," I bite out.

"You don't have to do that. Go, it's okay. I can hold down the fort."

I'm not going to let him win by leaving. I'm not going to let him get to me. I should be better than this, cooler than this. And yet the anger roils around in me, looking for a weak spot to burst through.

Rhys pushes me gently. "Go. I'll be fine on my own. Besides, your scowling is driving people away."

"People like my scowling."

"Not in person!"

I glance around us and goddamn it, Rhys is right. We

had a steady stream of fans coming up to The Camboy Network booth. But since Bellamy's interview started playing, an invisible perimeter has been erected around us. People are staying away, watching us warily like I might actually flip out on them. Cowards. All of them. "Fine. Call me if you need me to come back."

Rhys waves me off. "Yeah, yeah, I will. Now, get out of here before you scare all our fans off."

My escape from the main convention hall is slow. It's packed in there and I have to elbow my way through sometimes. A couple fans stop me beside a demonstration of a new blow-up doll and I make an effort to give them the signature and selfie they're looking for. Another group descends upon me next to some tech start-up debuting their latest porn app. I have to wave off bikini-clad girls handing out samples of condoms and lube. By the time I get out of there, I feel like I've taken a trek through Times Square.

Only to be greeted by a giant-ass billboard of Bellamy fucking Blais. His face is about two stories tall and he's staring down at me with an expression halfway between ecstasy and torture. His lips are parted like he's been breathing hard and his skin shines from a thin layer of sweat. It's a complete one-eighty from his typical fun-loving, easy-going, California surfer dude image, and for some reason it makes me stop and stare.

I feel that look of his skitter across my skin and then plunge deep into me. It coils through me, grasping my insides in its grip. Every muscle is on high alert, bracing for the physical tug I'm convinced is coming. But it doesn't. It keeps me waiting, primed, tense, the pressure building and building and building.

"Hi! Oh my god, are you Noel Carrington?"

The question snaps me out of my one-sided staring contest. There's a guy in front of me, clutching his phone to his chest.

"Holy shit, I'm such a huge fan. You have no idea."

I grind my anger under my heel and focus on being the celebrity crush this guy expects me to be. "Thanks. I love meeting my fans."

"Can I get a selfie?"

"Of course." I let him drape himself all over me as he snaps a couple shots. "Remember to tag me if you post that on social."

The guy's eyes light up. "Oh my god, I definitely will. Thank you so much!"

He slips into the crowd and I head for the nearest exit, making a point not to get caught up in Bellamy's giant face. Much good it does me when that same poster pops up to mock me around every corner. By the time I finally make it out of the hotel, that anger is prickling me from all sides again.

Five years on and our very public, very heated rivalry feels more potent now than it ever has before. Fans have divided themselves into Team Noel and Team Bellamy. There's a distinct east coast versus west coast vibe. There are entire sub/Reddits devoted to tracking every single thing we've ever said to or about each other. People can't get enough, and the dirtier it gets, the better.

*Is Noel's hair actually black? He probably dyes it to look cool.*

*I bet Bellamy takes Viagra to stay hard during shoots.*

*Noel needs some plastic surgery to fix his personality.*

*A potato can act better than Bellamy.*

*I feel bad for the guys who have to suck Noel's ugly cock.*

*Bellamy's gagging for my cock.*

I started it, I know that much. But the details of exactly when and how are a little hazy. It might have been that very night after I stumbled back to my hotel room in a rage. I have a vague memory of hate-scrolling his social media feed, already dripping with pictures of his magnificent victory. It would've been very in character for me if I'd made some acerbic comment on one of his photos.

The sun beats down on me from a cloudless blue sky as I stalk my way along the Strip. It's just as crowded out here as it was inside the hotel—people fucking everywhere, stopping in the middle of the goddamn sidewalk to take pictures of absolutely nothing.

I jump out onto the street to walk with the cars rather than weave my way around the pedestrians. Someone blares their horn at me and I return the sentiment with a middle finger. God, I really fucking hate Vegas.

———

Rhys isn't alone when I get back to our booth. Sebastian and Hayden are chatting with him, all three of them animated. And yet, they all fall silent when they spot me.

"What?"

Hayden and Rhys shuffle backward, leaving Sebastian looking hesitant and apologetic.

"Have you seen this?"

"Seen what?" I take Sebastian's phone from him and my stomach plummets when I see the screen.

It's a photo of me standing in the middle of the hall outside, staring up at Bellamy's oversized mug. The expression on my face is fierce and fiery. It could be anger or hatred or… obsession. An all-consuming, soul-eating obsession that has sunk its claws deep into me and is never letting me go.

Whoever took the photo deserves a fucking prize. I look possessed. But then, that's what it feels like sometimes. This thing has a life of its own, and it's so much bigger than me, sweeping me up in its wake. I'm caught in it, single-mindedly focused on it, and I can't escape it—I can't escape *him*.

I toss the phone back to Sebastian and when none of them speak, I bark out another "what?"

Hayden and Rhys spin away, but Sebastian cocks his head at me. "You okay?"

I fold my arms across my chest. "Yeah, why wouldn't I be?"

He opens his mouth, then wisely shuts it again. "Nothing. Never mind," he says with a quick squeeze of my shoulder. The touch communicates everything words can't.

I've sunk too deep into this. So deep that I won't be able to crawl out of it even if I want to. Well, jokes on all of them, because I've got a grudge, and I've got no intention of letting it go.

# CHAPTER
# TWO

## BELLAMY

The room is still dark when I open my eyes and it takes me a full five seconds to realize I'm not in my bed in San Francisco. It takes another five seconds for me to figure out I'm in Las Vegas. At the porn convention.

I groan, turn over, and bury my face in my pillow. Ew, my breath reeks. I flip onto my back and scrub a hand over my face.

Last night is a blur of flashing lights, thumping music, and the burn of alcohol down my throat. I don't remember what time I stumbled out of the nightclub and back to my hotel room. It couldn't have been more than a couple hours ago. And from the amount of glitter now permanently embedded in the sheets, it looks like I hadn't bothered to shower before collapsing and passing out.

Despite getting carted around by the executives over at Fetish Studios all day, and then "networking" at the clubs all night, I'm still wide awake before the sun has even touched the horizon. Old habits die hard, I guess, apparently even the good ones.

I roll out of bed and drag my feet into the bathroom to relieve myself, only to grimace when I flick on the light and catch a glimpse of my reflection in the mirror. I look like death warmed over, with bloodshot eyes and dull, splotchy skin. I rub the heels of my hands into my eyes and yeah, I feel worse than I look.

Everyone in the industry thinks of me as the bright, peppy one, always upbeat and never tired. If fans could see me now, I'm not sure they'd recognize me.

Mornings are my favorite time of day. Even now, as groggy as I am, moving on autopilot to change into old gym shorts and a tee, I can feel the quiet stillness in the air. Mornings smell nicer than midday when the rest of the world is up and about. It's lighter, thinner, like dew sprinkled on fresh-cut grass. It tickles my nose with every breath I take, it infuses every cell and chases away all the fatigue.

That early morning scent is stronger in the hallway and elevator. Something about being all alone in these spaces that are usually bustling with people. The normally stale air feels crisper when I'm the only person breathing it.

I keep my eyes mostly closed as I amble toward the hotel's fitness room and my daily morning run. When I'm at home, I run through the empty streets in my neighborhood. But when I'm away, hotel treadmills will do the trick. No matter where I am, though, getting my muscles pumping first thing in the day helps clear my mind and focuses me on what I need to do once the sun comes up.

Still half asleep, I don't notice the gym is occupied until I'm already inside. It takes me less than a second to recognize the tall, lithe frame, the pale skin, and the black hair. I don't need to see his face to know it's Noel Carrington.

Just my freaking luck.

I've always been able to spot Noel from across a crowded room. There's something about him that flashes like a lighthouse, drawing me in even as it warns me of the rocks below. He's like one of those guard dogs I've been warned to stay away from, but against my better judgment, I'll still reach out to pet him.

I swear I don't have a death wish. And I fully believe that Noel is capable of choosing violence if I push him too far. I guess I want to see how far I can push him—where is his line? And I'll be honest, watching him sputter and fume in public when I land a particularly good verbal jab is just about one of the most amusing pastimes ever invented.

It's hard to believe that we've been at each other's throats for five years and we've never actually been in the same room together. Not like this, just the two of us with no one else watching, no cameras perfectly focused to capture everything we say and do. I've always wondered whether Noel would be different in person. I mean, we're both wearing carefully crafted personas whenever we interact in public. But is Noel actually that arrogant and entitled and obnoxious in real life? No one can be that bad, right?

There are three treadmills in the fitness room, all lined up side-by-side, facing the window. Noel's running on the far left one and there's an "Out of Order" sign taped to the one closest to me. That leaves me with two options: suck it up and use the treadmill next to Noel's, or turn around and leave.

It's not really a choice.

I step up onto the treadmill, trying really hard to keep my shit-eating grin in check. I don't look in Noel's direction, but it's impossible to miss the moment he notices me. He does a sitcom-worthy double-take, then almost face-plants right into the running deck of the treadmill.

"You okay?" My question is accompanied by a barely contained snicker.

I can't help it. He's too funny. Standing on the two sides of the treadmill, glaring at me so hard I think he might pop a blood vessel.

"Fuck off." On a scale of endearing to murder, Noel's tone is about an eight.

I've no intention of going anywhere, and for a moment, he seems like he's going to leave instead. But then he turns to stare resolutely at the window and hops back onto the spinning belt. He's so damn grumpy I have to bite my lip to keep from laughing out loud.

I guess I was wrong. He might actually be as bad in person as he is in public. Which only makes me want to poke and prod at him more.

I hit the start button on my treadmill and gradually increase the speed to a light warm-up jog. My muscles and ligaments ease into the familiar motions of a run, loosening and lengthening as they wake up.

Out of the corner of my eye, I see Noel sneaking glances in my direction. He's pretty subtle, I have to give him that, but I'm so attuned to his every move that I can't miss it even if I want to. There's something about being this close to him, close enough to feel the heat coming off his body, to smell the sweat trailing down his skin. I find myself trying to match the rhythm of his feet, the steady in and out of his breathing. They both get thrown off whenever he slants his gaze toward me.

Gratification settles in my joints when the numbers on my screen match the numbers on his, when our synchronized footfalls echo through the room with a satisfying *thump, thump, thump.* The machines whir and blend into the gentle vibrations of air flowing through our tracheas, creating an oddly soothing background track. This is surprisingly nice, me and Noel, sitting in the groove, riding the wave.

Then he has to go fuck it up.

He hits the up arrow on his treadmill, yanking us out of tandem and sending a jolt of dissonance through me. A chuckle rumbles through my chest at how hard he jabs the speed controls. I should let him be surly and focus on my own workout, but let's be real, I'm just as bad as he is when it comes to trying to one-up each other. So he wants to go faster. Fine, I can go faster too. Faster than him, even, and his jaw ticks when he notices. He bumps up his speed. I give him a few seconds before bumping mine up higher.

Back and forth. Back and forth. Just like the insults we hurl at each other whenever there's the slightest chance someone can hear us. The need to be better, to prove we're better, to have the world acknowledge we're better, it's followed us onto these damn treadmills. We can't escape the competitiveness, not when it's so deeply engrained, when it's woven into the fabric of who we are.

My thighs burn. My lungs burn. My eyes sting from the sweat dripping into them. No matter how hard I pump my legs, I eventually start slipping toward the back of the running deck.

Nope. I'm not going to make it. My pride will have to

take the hit this time. I concede victory to the almighty Noel Carrington. It's not worth a trip to urgent care.

My palm makes contact with the emergency stop button a fraction of a second before I tumble off the tread-mill and land in a pile on the floor. I can't lift my arms or my head or untangle my legs. Bile trickles up my esophagus and I wince as I swallow it back down.

Noel comes off almost at the same time as me, catching himself on his hands and knees. His head hangs forward, hair sopping wet like he just stepped out of a shower. Our heaving breaths are the only sounds in the now-quiet fitness room.

He lifts his head to look at me. Glare at me. Bore holes into me. I've seen that expression of his before. Dozens of times. Hundreds of times. But never up close like this. Never when I could reach out and touch him, brush the hair off his forehead.

There's something in his eyes that I've never noticed before. An intensity that sucks me right in. He looks like he wants to kill me. Or kiss me. Or maybe he can't decide between the two. Either way, I'm caught in his stare, enthralled by him. My heart pounds against my ribs and a chill seeps into my bones. He's a predator and I'm his prey. He's going to consume me, it's merely a question of whether he'll toy with me first.

Then he blinks and the moment is gone. He's still got daggers shooting out of his eyes, but for the moment they're directed at the grungy carpet rather than at me.

"What the fuck are you doing here anyway?" he asks, moving to sit against the wall.

I drag myself to the opposite wall and sprawl out until

I'm mostly lying on the floor. "Seriously?" I snort. "What does it look like I'm doing?"

"Annoying the fuck out of me."

"News flash, jerk face, not everything's about you."

Noel stews, jaw ticking, lips all screwed up. I'm surprised he's still sitting there. I would have expected him to bolt by now, not sit here with me, close enough that our feet could touch if I angled mine in the right direction. But he doesn't look like he's moving anytime soon.

And well, if he's not leaving, then neither am I. Because suddenly I'm curious—maybe there *is* something more to Noel than his perpetual bad mood.

**CHAPTER**
# THREE

**NOEL**

Not everything's about me? Well, not everything's about him either, asshole.

Except sometimes it is. Especially when I'm minding my own business and in walks Bellamy Blais and his goddamn smirk of a smile. Then all I can think about is the way his muscles bunch and flex as he moves, the smattering of glitter on his arm, the whiff of coconut sunscreen and sweat that reminds me of a sunny day at the beach.

Even now, seeing him sprawled out on the floor, long limbs splayed haphazardly, utterly undignified, I have this unfathomable urge to crawl over and… I don't know. Touch him or something. Lick him. Grab him and shake him and… Jesus Christ, what the hell is wrong with me? I hate the guy—fine. I want to see him crash and burn— cool. But the reactions he whips up in me are so all-consuming, so wildly out of control that sometimes I feel like I'm physically drowning in them.

It doesn't help that he's looking at me through half-lidded eyes, plump lips parted with a hint of a curl. He's laughing at me. I can hear it even though he hasn't made a single sound. He's assessing me. It crawls across my skin.

"Fuck you," I say because I can't think of anything else, because I need to say something or else I might crawl across this disgusting carpet and do something I'll regret later.

The insult rolls off him as he chuckles, shoulders shaking. It fades into a sigh that's smug and resigned. "What are you doing up so early anyway?"

The dumbass question catches me off guard and I cock an eyebrow. He knows where I live. "New York is three hours ahead, genius."

He nods, slow and lazy, like maybe his head isn't screwed onto his neck tightly enough. He drags his foot across the carpet until it's flat on the floor, his knees high enough for him to prop his arm on. The leg of his gym shorts slides to the top of his thigh and the edge of his briefs peak out. Bright yellow—like the fucking sun.

"I'm surprised you're here," Bellamy says, casually, conversationally, as if we're old friends reuniting for the first time in years, and not age-old enemies who can't stand to be in the same room together. "At the convention, I mean. I thought you didn't like this stuff."

I tear my eyes away from Bellamy's crotch, scowling at the amusement dancing on his face. He's only partially right—I don't like big, showy productions like this. At least not when I'm not the star of the show. If it were my face plastered all over the hotel, though? I'm never going to say no to that level of public adoration.

"What makes you think I don't like conventions?"

Bellamy's shoulder lifts a fraction of an inch, then

drops down again. "I read it somewhere."

"You can read?"

He laughs out loud this time, face splitting in a grin, and he almost topples over sideways. "Fuck you, Carrington. You think you're so funny."

I don't, actually, think I'm funny, that is. I'm a dark, brooding bad boy. "I am funny. I'm hilarious."

Bellamy rolls his eyes, but he's still smiling so it comes across as indulgent, appeasing, fond. "Yeah, sure you are."

Goddamn asswipe. I want to scrub that smugly superior look off his face—preferably with my dick.

But then Bellamy tilts his head in puzzlement. "Why do you hate me so much, anyway? Did I kick your puppy or something?"

Is he joking? How can he not know? Is he trying to bait me into something? I snarl at him and for once, his expression grows wary.

"It's not because I won that year, is it?" He sounds apologetic, like his heart goes out to the novice who doesn't know any better. "I know that's what people say, but you can't be that petty."

Yeah, well, I guess I fucking am. I surge to my feet and Bellamy follows me up like he doesn't want to be caught unprepared if I advance on him. Smart move—for once—because I stalk up to him and shove him with both hands on his chest.

His eyes go wide with shock and his brow furrows in disbelief. "Dude, what the hell?"

Satisfaction trickles through my veins, fueling my bubbling anger. "You think you're such a big fucking deal, so goddamn important. Mr. Golden Boy, who everyone loves to fawn over."

"What the fuck are you talking about?"

"You think you've got everyone fooled, don't you? With your fake tan and even faker smile. 'Oh, look at me, I'm Bellamy Blais, I'm god's fucking gift to the planet. I'm so goddamn special. Everyone's begging to suck my dick.'"

"Are you serious right now?"

"I see through your little farce. You're nothing more than a fake, a sham, a fraud. You're a conniving, manipulative piece of shit, and I don't believe one second of the happy-go-lucky act you put on for the cameras."

He shoves me. Hard. Hands to my chest, burning through the thin fabric of my shirt and scalding my skin underneath. I stumble backward and even though he's not touching me anymore, the imprint of his hands are two raw, scorched patches.

"You're unbelievable. You don't know a single fucking thing about me. I'm just playing the game you started—" He drives his point home by jabbing his finger into my chest. I smack it away from me. "—with all your shit-talking and unprovoked insults. You're arrogant and bitter, and you can't stomach the idea that I *am* better than you and there's nothing you can fucking do about it."

*We're the same height.*

We're nose-to-nose, micro-seconds away from an all-out physical brawl, and *that's* the thought that races through my mind. I always assumed Bellamy was taller than me, and for some irrational reason, that rankles me. So fucking cheerful all the time. Beloved by the whole goddamn world. *And* he's taller? Can't I win at just one thing?

But standing here with him in my face, eyes staring

murder, an illogical sense of pride makes me stand up straighter. He's not taller than me, he's exactly my height. We're on the same level, we're evenly matched. It's one less thing he can lord over me. One more thing I've stripped away from him.

Bellamy exhales hot puffs of air over my chin. That coconut sunscreen and salty sweat scent fills my nose and winds its way through me. His blue eyes have dozens of thin white spokes emanating from the pupil like a sun-shaped snowflake. His bottom lip is so full it almost curls over on itself, leaving a tiny dip under it, right in the middle—perfect for catching my teeth on as I bite into the soft, plump flesh.

Will he moan? Will he gasp? Will he cling to me, begging me for more? Or will he fight me for control? My cock is at half-mast and quickly growing harder.

*Jesus.*

"You know, you think you're such a tough guy, such a badass," he says, whispery and taunting. "But I'm starting to think it's all an act." He tilts his head and pushes his bottom lip out in a mocking pout. "I think underneath all this big, scary macho man is a sensitive, scared little boy."

My simmering rage boils over. I grab him, fisting my hands in his shirt, hauling him even closer to me so I can shut him the fuck up. Bellamy's eyes flash with a challenge, a dare. His tongue sneaks out to wet his lip, then he tilts his chin up like he's offering his mouth to me.

"Go on, Carrington. What are you going to do?" His words are a punch to my gut.

I stumble backward, pushing him away from me. I was *this close* to kissing him, and even now my veins thrum with the urge to crash my body into his. There's not a shred of doubt in my mind that it'd be blistering, searing, combustible. My cock is on board, hard as a rock, even as ugly resentment creeps up on me.

Bellamy fucking Blais, with his perfect fucking lips and startlingly clear blue eyes. That curl of damp hair falling over his forehead begging me to run my fingers through it. The sharp edge of his sugar-coated words. How dare he look so effortlessly composed when I'm all turned around inside?

Bellamy's eyes narrow a fraction, a minuscule tightening of muscles, and his lips part like he has more to say. But then, he closes them and smiles at me like something's occurred to him. He fucking smiles like some puzzle piece has finally fallen into place. His gaze travels down the length of my body, leaving a trail of heat in its wake. My heart almost arrests with how hard it's trying to pump blood to my dick.

Does he feel it too? The current arcing between us, making the air crackle and sizzle? Half my face tingles from the phantom spark of a phantom kiss. I can almost feel the shape of his mouth against mine, the slide of our tongues as we duel it out, the rasp of his stubble. I can almost taste the sunshine on his skin.

I'm losing my ever-loving mind. He's cast an unholy spell on me, making me think things I shouldn't be thinking, wanting things I have no place to want.

I scramble a few more steps, tripping over some loose strands of carpet in my hurry to get out. I need to get away from him, as far as I can possibly go, before I do something truly shit-brained, something I can't take back—like kiss Bellamy fucking Blais.

# CHAPTER
# FOUR

## BELLAMY

For someone who supposedly hates me, Noel sure does follow me around a lot. Everywhere I've been today, every panel and signing and photo op, I keep seeing him at the back of the room, or at the edge of a crowd, just close enough to maintain line of sight. He's always got his arms crossed, feet planted wide, a scowl etched on his face.

It's gotten to the point where I don't really need to look for him anymore. All I have to do is stop for a moment and I'll be able to sense where he is, like I've got a radar tuned specifically to Noel's frequency. Maybe it's the weight of his stare, boring into my face, or the potency of his disapproval, thickening the air.

Every time I look up and our gazes collide, a bolt of lightning ricochets between us. Like that moment in the fitness room, standing toe-to-toe, barely an inch between us, the air suddenly felt charged enough to power a lightbulb. And he grabbed me and I was sure that we'd light the oxygen on fire.

I guess that's what makes us great rivals. The animosity between us is so electric that we'd risk starting a fire if left together for too long. Or, to be accurate, Noel hates me. I'm not a fan of the guy—he's unpleasant, arrogant, and entitled—but I have no reason to actually hate him.

I was honest with him this morning: I don't know what I've done to warrant his loathing. As far as I can tell, we were complete strangers, I edged him out on the Best Newcomer award, and suddenly he's jumping down my throat. The rumors are that he's upset he lost out to me. And based on his reaction this morning, that could be it.

It's kind of ridiculous if it is. I mean, someone had to win and it's not like it's the Oscars or anything. It's a porn award, for god's sake. People win because they've got big dicks. If it means so much to him, he can have the damn thing. It's just collecting dust on a shelf in my room anyway.

Whatever his motives, I do have to thank Noel for launching the rivalry between us. I don't know if I would get half as much attention from the media and from fans without it. And believe me, I need all the publicity I can get. People get into camming for all sorts of reasons, but mine is pretty textbook—I need the money.

So yeah, I don't believe half the things I lob in Noel's direction. Sometimes I make shit up because I know it'll hit a sore spot and get a rise out of him. It's entertaining to watch Noel fume all the time, sputtering around while he tries to find a way to strike back at me.

There are times, though, when his hostility gets old. Like, isn't it exhausting being that angry all the time? Shit. I get tired just watching him sulk and seethe. The thing is, I'm not convinced that's actually who he is. There were a couple moments this morning when I thought I saw his mask slip. Like when we fell off the treadmills and landed in a pile of arms and legs on the floor. Or when he grabbed my shirt and hauled me to him. It wasn't anger that I read in his eyes—or at least, it wasn't only anger.

There's another ten minutes before I need to be at my next event, so I steal away from the Fetish Studio executives who have been shuttling me around and get some air.

I don't usually work with studios and I don't usually do anything kinky. But their offer of an edging video was too good to turn down, and with the amount of resources and effort they're putting into marketing the video, I'm going to end up making a killing. Hence the non-stop smiling at fans, answering the same questions over and over again, and getting assaulted by images of my own face everywhere I turn. I can barely stand seeing it plastered all over the place, I can only imagine what everyone else is feeling.

The out-of-the-way restroom I find is at the end of a deserted hallway, far from the noise and crowds of the convention. Except it seems like fate or god or someone is conspiring against us because the restroom is not empty— it's populated by one Noel Carrington. Twice in one day. I don't know how I managed to get so lucky.

Noel is standing by the sinks and he spins around the moment he catches sight of me in the mirrors. "What the fuck are you doing here? Are you following me?"

I burst out laughing, not on purpose, but you have to appreciate the irony of the situation. "You tell me. You've been lurking in every single room I've walked into today, so maybe *you're* following *me*?"

Noel scoffs and slides into his defensive, arms-crossed pose. "Trust me. If I could've avoided you, I would have. It's obnoxious that you're everywhere."

"Obnoxious? Or impressive." I make sure to smirk and cock an eyebrow. I can't help it. It's too easy.

His eyes burn and his jaw ticks. One of these days, the top of his head is going to blow right off with the amount of pressure building in there. I can only hope to witness it when it happens.

I saunter by him, close enough to nudge his shoulder with my own, and I'm rewarded with a not-so-subtle, "Fucker."

My back is turned while I do my business at the last urinal in the row, but that almost makes Noel's scowl that much more visceral. I can practically feel the waves of fury rolling off him. I can almost hear the whistle signaling that his top is about to explode.

He's barely moved when I go to wash my hands.

"What are you hiding from?" I ask, though I don't know why I bother.

"I'm not hiding from anything."

I roll my eyes. "Oh yeah? Then why did you go out of your way to find the most obscure restroom in the hotel?"

"Why did *you* go out of your way to find the most obscure restroom?"

I sigh. I shouldn't have asked. I turn and rest my hip against the counter.

Noel's got black leather cuffs on both wrists, heavy black boots on his feet, and the tightest pair of leather pants I've ever set my eyes on. The outline of his dick is so prominent, he could use the damn thing as a printing press.

His shirt is one of those black mesh things that's almost see-through. He might as well be shirtless. There's a simple silver bar pierced through his left nipple and I have a sudden, inexplicable urge to run my tongue over it, catch it on my teeth, and tug. Would there be a spark upon contact? Like when you stick your tongue into an electrical socket? Would Noel gasp at the scrape of my teeth? Would he moan as his dick strains against the too-tight fabric of his pants?

I shake my head, trying to erase the images my overactive imagination is insistent upon feeding to me.

"I'm here probably for the same reason you are—to get away from all that." I wave in the general direction of the convention. My voice is impressively neutral. Not a hint of drama in it. Look at me, I'm a mature adult.

But when Noel doesn't answer, I push away from the counter and head for the door. If he doesn't want to engage, then fine. I don't have any extra energy to waste on arguing with him today.

I make it two steps before running into an immovable object called Noel. He glares at me with those dark eyes and it takes a microsecond for me to fall into their bottomless pools. I can't look away, too caught up in studying the various shades of brown and black as they swirl around in circles. They're hypnotizing, and I'm enthralled.

Awareness spreads through me as I imagine Noel forcing me to my knees with nothing more than a look. Of Noel sliding his cock past my lips and down my throat. Of Noel pinning me to the bed, spread open and exposed.

Blood rushes to my dick so fast I sway on my feet.

Noel notices. His eyes widen in understanding, then drop to the front of my pants—also too tight. And goddamn, if that doesn't cause goosebumps to break out all over my freaking body.

My cock grows under his scrutiny, and his lips part as an almost imperceptible shudder rushes through him. Is he feeling this too? This electricity zinging between us?

I take a step forward, and gratification surges through me at Noel's quick intake of breath. Oh yeah, he's feeling it. His nipples are pebbled into hard nubs, and that outline in his leather pants is significantly longer and thicker than it had been a moment ago.

I take another step forward, silently daring Noel to back down, to deny this volatile energy sparking between us. He doesn't move, and satisfaction hums in my belly. Then his gaze shoots up to mine. They've hardened into solid black orbs. He's angry. He's vibrating with it.

"What are you doing?" Noel spits out.

"I could ask you the same thing." I pitch my voice low so it doesn't echo off the walls. "You're the one standing in my way."

And still, Noel doesn't move.

*Kiss me. Come on, kiss me.*

The thought almost startles me out of this game of chicken we're playing. I've never denied that Noel is an attractive man, that I find him attractive. And there was that moment this morning when his lips were less than a fraction away from mine. But I've never had such a clear and explicit craving for him, for his mouth, for his hands. I've never wanted to act on my attraction this badly, or been tempted to push Noel into acting on his.

He wants to kiss me. I can tell from the buzz of current

in the air, from the way Noel's breaths are coming short and fast. He's going to do it. I'm sure of it.

Then he doesn't. He steps back. Fucking coward.

Noel blinks like he's waking up from some hypnotic state and only now realizing where he is and who he's with. And here I thought *I* had gotten hypnotized. Disappointment, stronger than I could have anticipated, crashes into me. I really fucking wanted him to kiss me. I wanted him to lose control, to go wild and feral on me.

I still want that, and my brain makes a decision before I can stop it.

I reach into the back pocket of my shorts and feel for the hard plastic card. I'm probably going to regret this tomorrow. Hell, I'm probably going to regret it the second I step outside this damn restroom. But right now, there's nothing that can stop me from holding the card up between my fore and middle fingers.

"Room 2215." I toss the card on the counter and walk out.

# CHAPTER
# FIVE

## NOEL

I notice him the second he steps foot inside the packed, noisy nightclub. Even if I'm not on high alert for Bellamy all the freaking time, it's impossible to miss the giant entourage he's at the head of.

I clutch the glass in my hand and watch the procession move across the dance floor to my side of the club. It's dark in here, lit only by the roaming, colored lights and disco balls. And yet, I can see Bellamy as clearly as if he was standing under the midday sun. It's like there's a fucking spotlight following him around everywhere, making sure he's the center of everyone's fucking attention.

God, I can't wait to get out of this hellhole and back to New York. I toss back the rest of my whiskey and slam the glass down on the table harder than necessary.

"You okay?" Hayden asks, glancing at the glass, then up at me. He and Rhys are coming off the dance floor, sweaty and smiling, and looking for all the world like they're having the time of their lives.

Meanwhile, I'm sitting here, warming the seats of the VIP booth hosted by a dildo company Sebastian's trying to close a deal with. He's on the other side of the table, shouting into the CEO's ear—something about making silicon replicas of our dicks, I'm sure.

Hayden cocks a concerned eyebrow in my direction, but Rhys jumps in before I can figure out how to express my extreme and utter frustration over this entire trip.

"Over there!" Rhys nods toward the table at the far end of the row where Bellamy and his crew are settling in.

"Oh. Shit."

Yeah. Shit is right. Total bullshit.

Hayden and Rhys shoot me matching sympathetic looks.

"Want another drink?" Rhys asks.

"Yes, many."

They flag down a waiter, then collapse onto the padded bench next to some employees of the dildo company. No one tries to draw me into a conversation. I'm not interested in screaming over the thumping music anyway.

A few tables away, Bellamy lets himself be dragged out onto the dance floor by the two guys he did the edging video with. The crowd parts for them like there's some invisible bow breaking through the water, then closes back up behind them. They take center stage, Bellamy sandwiched between two hunks who have more muscles than brains, and the three of them move like they're one person. Everyone watches—it's impossible not to. The way Bellamy throws his head back, the look of ecstatic delight on his face. Those hands on his body, touching him, gliding over his skin, digging into his flesh.

My cock twitches and stirs at the sight of them—of Bellamy—as they grind up on each other, oblivious to the music, to the audience they've captured. They're lost in their own little world where the only thing that exists is how they make each other feel.

None of it is real. It's all a publicity stunt, and it's working. Flashes from cell phone cameras compete with nightclub lights, every single one pointed at Bellamy and his doms. Those photos are pouring onto the internet in real time, and before the night is over, everyone and their mother will know what Bellamy looks like on the dance floor.

I know the whole thing is staged. But that doesn't stop me from staring all the same.

Someone steps in front of me and I growl in irritation as I lose sight of Bellamy. I try to look around the guy, but it's the waiter, trying to hand me the drink I ordered. I grab it from him and wave him away. My unease dissolves the second I zero in on Bellamy again.

Except this time, he's not quite as lost in the music and his dancing partners. His eyes are open, and they're locked on me.

I forget to breathe.

He's got his hooks in me, lodged deep in my gut, and he's slowly reeling me in, ripping through my insides while he's at it. It's a physical pull that's got me on the edge of my seat, and I have to brace my feet to stop myself from standing up and marching right onto the dance floor.

*To do what? Kiss him? Punch him?*

Fuck if I know. But the challenge in his eyes is irresistible and the pain of not responding is palpable.

Hayden and Rhys are on their feet again.

"We're going to dance. Come with us!" Rhys grabs my hand and gives it a shake. "You can stop staring at Bellamy and show everyone that you've got better moves than him."

I glare up into Rhys's teasing expression and slump back into my seat, dislodging my hand from his. "I don't dance."

Rhys rolls his eyes. "Yeah, I know, I know. You're too cool to dance. You just sit there, looking dark and dangerous." His tone is light enough that I know he's joking, barely. "Fine, have it your way. *We* are going to have fun!"

He and Hayden link arms and disappear onto the dance floor. When I turn my attention back to Bellamy, he's still watching me, this time with a smirk on his lips. Like he knows what Rhys had said. Like he knows I won't dare get up and dance.

Fucker.

One of his dancing partners grips Bellamy's hair and wrenches it back so the other can run his lips up Bellamy's neck. His jaw drops open and his eyes drift shut, and my cock is doing its best to burst out of my pants.

I shift to adjust and a hard piece of plastic pokes me in the ass. Bellamy's room key. It's been burning a hole through my pocket all day. That scene in the bathroom has played itself out over and over in my mind, each time bringing me right to the brink, that knife's edge between wanting him and hating him that slices me straight through. He drives me out of my fucking mind with those clear blue eyes and that plump bottom lip, teasing me, taunting me, daring me to do something I'm sure I'm going to regret. And as much as I try, as much as I tell myself I want to, I can't seem to shake him loose.

What am I supposed to do with his room key? What had Bellamy been thinking when he gave it to me? That I'd show up and we'd... talk? Fight? Fuck? Lust surges through me at the image of us together, naked, hands gripping, bodies crashing, teeth sinking into flesh. It's so powerful, it's debilitating, leaving me shuttering and weak.

Bellamy slips out from between his two meatheads and weaves his way back to his table. He accepts a drink from one person and takes his time talking with another. His smile never wavers. People fawn over him. He's every inch the golden boy and they all play right into his hands.

There's something wrong with me. There has to be. I've hated this guy for five years and now suddenly I want to fuck him? Now I can't stop fantasizing about sinking into his heat while pinning him to the bed, the sounds he'll make as I touch him, and the look on his face when he comes.

As if he can hear my thoughts, Bellamy looks my way again. It's hard to make out with all the flashing lights and heads getting in the way, but I swear there's something in his eyes. It's calling my name, luring me in.

I stand. His lips twitch. Across the distance, with people and music and lights all around us, a message travels from him to me. I can hear it plain as day, as if he whispered it right into my ear. *Coming?*

My stomach lurches as it tries to follow him out the door. My feet stumble forward a few steps before I catch myself. Am I really doing this? Show up at Bellamy's door in the middle of the night for god knows what reason? My heart pounds in my chest, and the sound of blood rushing past my ears drowns out everything until all I can hear is the faint echo of his question.

"Noel! Where are you going?" Sebastian's voice trickles into my mind but is quickly dismissed. There's only one thing I need to do right now, one place I need to be.

The dry midnight air of Las Vegas hits my sweat-damp skin and goosebumps break out down my arms. Bellamy's nowhere in sight. But that's okay, I know where to find him, I know where he's going.

It doesn't take long for me to make it back to our hotel, then up to the twenty-second floor.

*2212, 2213, 2214.*

I stop in front of Bellamy's door and reach into my pocket for the keycard. When I pull it out, something about the hard plastic, warm from where it's been sitting next to my body all day, snaps me out of whatever thrall Bellamy put me in and I finally come to my senses.

I must be delusional, coming to Bellamy's room like this. Nothing good can come from it. I should walk away now before I do something I can't undo. I grip the card until its edges dig into my palm. If I turn around now, he won't even have to know I was here. We can both pretend none of this happened.

I spin on my heel, but before I can take a single step, the sound of metal locks tumbling against metal stops me in my tracks. The door opens, and there he is.

# CHAPTER
# SIX

## BELLAMY

I knew he would come. I knew it the second I got to the nightclub and realized Noel was there too. The smolder in his eyes, heavy and hot on me the entire time, burning me up from across the room. It was too perfect. I couldn't have arranged it better if I'd done it on purpose.

If I ground up against my two co-stars a little more raunchily than I'd planned, and if I let them grope me and rub me all over, I couldn't be blamed. My heart fluttered in my chest every time I glanced toward Noel and found his scowl growing deeper and fiercer. He hated that I was there. He hated that his eyes were drawn to me and that he couldn't tear them away. I loved that he was so obsessed, despite himself.

And now he's here, like I'd known he would be. Standing there with his furrowed brow and lips twisted into a snarl, confusion and anger pouring off him at the same time. He looks so pained, like he's here under duress, like someone's holding a gun to his head. Poor guy.

I almost want to take pity on him and send him away. Say this whole thing was a mistake, a misunderstanding. I hadn't meant to give him my room key. I hadn't wanted him to show up at my door. He can leave and go back to his friends or wherever and we can forget any of this ever happened. I'm *this close* to actually apologizing to the guy when something snaps in him.

Suddenly, he's through the door, crashing into me, shoving me up against the wall. His mouth slams into mine so hard we could both end up bleeding. His teeth close over my bottom lip and he bites into it, tugging at it like he's going to rip right through the flesh, and Jesus Christ, my cock must have a fucked-up sense of what's hot because it's raging at the pain and fear coursing through me at Noel's attack.

He plunges his tongue into my mouth like he's trying to choke me with it, and there's nothing I can do but moan around the thick, dexterous muscle. His hands clamp onto both sides of my face, holding me at the exact angle he needs to keep ravaging my mouth. I've never been kissed like this before, like he's trying to kill me, like he's trying to suck the oxygen straight out of my lungs.

Whatever expectations I had about what happens after Noel shows up, whatever scenarios my imagination dreamed up about us, it all pales in comparison to the real thing. He's so much more intense, so much more over-whelming than when he's filtered through the internet. He's demanding and insistent, and he won't take no for an answer.

He wants me with a ferocity that can't be ignored. It's

in the way his fingers dig into my scalp, how his body molds to mine, the hard bulge pressing into my hip. He wants me even when he doesn't want to want me, and that's making him all the more frenzied.

Just as quickly as he ambushed me, he throws himself back. Chest heaving, eyes wild, lips red and wet from our mouth wrestling. He looks like he's in shock, like he's not sure how he got here or what he's been doing. He looks like he's about to bolt.

I can't have that. Not when I've only just managed to get my hands on him. When my cock is demanding the release it's been promised and that it's determined to get.

I advance upon Noel and he retreats. One step, then two. Until he hits the edge of the bed with the back of his knees. I've got him trapped. He's got nowhere else to go but down.

He trains his dark eyes on me, watching every move I make with alarm and distrust. If I put my fingers to his throat, his pulse will be through the fucking roof. He's taut and tense, hands curled into fists—maybe because he wants to punch me, or maybe to stop himself from grabbing me again.

I pause when we're toe-to-toe. We've been finding ourselves in this position a lot lately, and I have to admit, I kind of like it. We're evenly matched. Same height, similar build, both too stubborn for our own good. Facing off with him feeds some competitive part of me that I hadn't known existed before we launched into our rivalry. But now that it's awakened, it needs to be fed—by Noel.

I run a finger over my lip, gingerly poking at the sore spot where his teeth have left indentations. "You bit me."

His gaze drops to my mouth and a look of triumph comes over his face. "You deserved it."

"Maybe I should return the favor."

He scoffs. "I'd like to see you try."

Challenge accepted. I pounce on him, and the momentum sends us tumbling onto the bed. I go at his mouth just as aggressively as he kissed mine, lots of teeth, driving tongue, spit flying and mixing until our lips are so wet, they're slipping and sliding off each other.

I've got one arm curled around the top of his head, fingers in his hair. My other hand slips under that gauzy barely there shirt he's wearing and clamps onto his waist. He bucks under me, not hard enough to dislodge me, but enough for his erection to rock up against mine. We both groan into each other's mouths and our tongue battle is forgotten as we shift our attention. I roll my hips, his hands come to my ass, I brush my already tender lips across his stubbled jaw and let out a strangled, "Fuck," right into his ear.

Noel takes advantage of my momentary weakness and flips us over. Air whooshes out of my lungs at the unexpected change in position and my head spins from lack of blood. It's all converged down in my cock, and whatever is left in my circulatory system is headed there too, especially when Noel sits up, knees on either side of me, and pulls his shirt off.

His nipple ring glints as he moves and I surge off the bed to suck it into my mouth. Noel hisses, stabs his fingers into my hair, and holds me to him as I work the metal bar with my tongue. It's warm—I don't know why I assumed it would be cool when it's literally pierced through his body. But something about the heat of the hard nubs at the ends of the bar makes me shudder when I brush my lips over them. It's a part of him, and yet it's not. It's a foreign object that shouldn't be there, melded into his skin.

When I latch onto it with my teeth and tug, Noel lets out a high-pitched, shaky cry, like he thinks I'm going to rip the bar right out. He curls in around me, wrapping his arms around the back of my head, my shoulders. His cock pulses against my stomach. I guess it likes the danger just as much as mine does.

I soothe the tortured nipple with my tongue, only letting go when Noel starts scrabbling to get my shirt off. We pull it over my head together and Noel flings it aside, then he grabs my face to fuck me with his tongue again.

My fingers fumble at the clasp of his leather pants, and when I peel the two sides apart, I realize the fucker has been walking around commando the whole fucking day. His cock fills my entire hand, long and thick and leaking like a hose. The smell of his pre-cum fills my nose, potent and musky and mouthwatering.

"Oh fuck," Noel mutters, releasing my mouth to drop his head back.

I rub my thumb back and forth over that spot under the head, then slide it up into his slit. A gush of pre-cum rushes over my thumb and I lean in to lick it up. It tastes better than it smells—strong and earthy and intoxicating. I chase it, taking his cock between my lips and sucking.

Noel's fingers tighten in my hair, his hips jut forward, though I don't think he does it on purpose. He's acting on instinct, his body moving according to some evolutionary need to chase pleasure. I understand. I'm doing the same, taking more and more of him until he's lodged in my throat and my nose is jammed up against his pelvis. I palm his balls, they're weighty and swollen in my hand, and when I slip my fingers back, they brush against something that's unnaturally hard.

I freeze. Is that…? It is. It's a fucking piercing. A ring this time, through his perineum with a bead hanging from it. The metal feels heavy as I trace my finger along the curve. It swings and I can see in my mind how it would slam into the back of Noel's balls as he fucks someone.

*As he fucks me.*

My hole clenches at the thought. How hard would Noel have to drive into me to get that ring to hit just right? The pain must be exquisite on his tender, sensitive sac.

"Intrigued?"

I pull off Noel's dick and peer up at him through my lashes. He's smirking, the bastard. How did I not know he had a ring back there? I've watched his videos before—I've studied them—and I've never seen it. I would remember if I had.

Well, now's my chance for a close-up.

I take the waistband of his pants and tug, but they're too damn tight to get off like this. I grab Noel and flip us over so I'm on top. When he's on his back, I peel the pants off him. Shoes and socks and clothes all land somewhere on the floor, mine included, before I climb back onto the bed between Noel's legs. I'm determined to see that piercing, to get it in my mouth and discover all the various reactions I can elicit from Noel.

My lips land on the piercing and Noel's hips come right off the bed. His fingertips rake over my scalp. His cries are a symphony to my ears and I can change his pitch by how hard I suck and tug on the ring.

"Fuck! Fuck! You bastard!"

I smile with my face still buried between his legs and glance past his balls and cock, all the way up his body. He's enraged. Cheeks red, brows so furrowed they form a single line, mouth curled into a snarl. His face is screaming at me to get off him, but the rest of him is sending me a very different message. Noel's cock is rock hard and there's a growing pool of pre-cum on his stomach. He keeps thrusting his hips at me, clawing at my head to keep me where I am. His brain might be furious that we're here, doing this, but some deeper, more primal part of him loves it.

That's what's so fascinating about this man, this struggle he's found himself caught in. He doesn't under-stand it, that much is obvious, but I have a feeling I might.

With one last flick of his perineum, I start working my way up—balls, cock, the flat plane of his abs, the hard pebbles of his nipples, the long length of his neck. By the time I get back to his mouth, he's shaking with need, with barely restrained lust.

He flips us over again and I cede control to him. He catches my jaw with one hand as he kisses me, rough and raw. With his other, he holds our erections together. Hard as steel and velvety soft at the same time. So hot it feels like it's been heated in a furnace. He thrusts against me, the head of his cock catching on the ridge of mine and a shock of pleasure rushes through me.

My hands go to his ass, squeezing and pulling, urging him on as we rub and grind against each other. We're sprinting toward the finish line together, racing to see who will get there first, who can hold off the longest. He beats me—or I beat him, who the hell knows—and his whole body jerks as he empties himself all over my stomach. The molten heat of it, hot and wet, pushes me over the edge and I add to the mess of cum squelching between us.

Noel collapses on me, face buried in the crook of my neck. His breath is a damp stirring of air against my sweat-soaked skin. I flatten my palms against the lean muscles of his back and press my lips to the top of his head. We lay there, floating on our shared post-orgasmic bliss.

Jesus Christ. A smile graces my lips. I just had sex with Noel fucking Carrington. Really fucking hot sex. Better than anything I've had recently—hell, it might be better than anything I've ever had. I'm not surprised though. All these years of sniping at each other, of bickering and throwing insults back and forth, it was bound to result in something explosive. The pressure can only build for so long before it needs to escape. And escape spectacularly, it did.

Noel goes still. His body stiffens, switching to high alert. All traces of languid satisfaction vanish in an instant and suddenly, he's pushing himself off me. He flies off the bed, stumbling backward like he hadn't known what he was doing or who he was doing it with.

I prop myself up on my elbows to watch him freak out. He doesn't disappoint. His fingers are in his hair, tugging like he might rip the strands right out of his scalp. Then he's scrambling for his clothes. It's comical, watching him try to squeeze himself into those too-tight leather pants. He does it somehow, hopping around and cursing up a storm. I have to bite my lip to keep from commenting. Something tells me that no matter what I say, it's not going to go over well.

Noel doesn't bother with his shirt or his socks or his shoes. He simply gathers them all up in his arms and hurries for the door. I expect him to wrench it open and throw himself into the hallway, but he stops. Hand on the doorknob, chest heaving, either from his frantic dressing or from a pending panic attack. He turns his head halfway to speak over his shoulder.

"This didn't happen."

Then he's gone.

I flop back on the bed, a grin firmly planted on my face. Noel's wrong. This did indeed happen. I've got a stomach covered in cum to prove it.

# CHAPTER
# SEVEN

## NOEL

The water pressure in my shower is amazing, so high that my face and chest sting a bit as I stand underneath it. It's exactly what I need: a good power wash to strip all traces of Las Vegas from my body.

All traces of Bellamy Blais.

It's been more than twenty-four hours since that misguided decision to go to his hotel room and I can still feel the shape of him against me. I can still taste him on my tongue, smell that coconut sunscreen, salty air, and sunshine-y scent of his skin. If I close my eyes, I feel like I'm back in the room again, on that bed again, his mouth on my nipple, his tongue flicking my piercing.

My hand drifts there now, toying with the metal bar, the same way Bellamy had. I pinch and tug and a zing of pleasure shoots straight to my cock. I give myself a few lazy strokes, my dick quickly filling at the memory of his mouth. So hot. So tight. The way he took me all the way down his throat without a single flinch.

Then his mouth on my guiche. Oh, fucking god. The rush of blood straight to my cock makes my head spin and I slap a hand on the shower wall to brace myself as my body jolts and convulses. I'm not going to come from a memory. That's ridiculous. No matter how good the sex was.

Except, I can still feel the seal of his lips on my skin. The negative pressure as he sucked. The way the ring moved, almost like it was right up inside me, hitting my balls, my ass, and my prostate all at the same time.

I lean my forehead against the cool tiles of the wall, freeing up my hand to reach back. I toy with the ring, tug it away from me, pinch the skin around it. My other hand is flying over my cock, fast and tight, and my whole body is taut in anticipation.

The look of surprise on Bellamy's face when I flipped us over and pinned him down. Him yielding to me, handing over control, letting me take charge of our mutual pleasure. The way he sucked on my tongue when I jammed it into his mouth. The way he grabbed my ass to ask for more, more, more.

I paint my shower wall with cum as all those images—those memories—of Bellamy flood through my mind. My body, my skin, hell, even my face tingles with the force of my orgasm.

Going to Bellamy's hotel room was a colossal mistake. Now I know what he feels like, what he tastes like, what he looks like when he comes. I can't un-know those things. They're burned into my brain forever and I'm going to have to live with those memories. They're going to haunt me day in and day out. I'm fucked.

I'm sluggish as I turn the water off and reach for a

towel. Morning shower hand jobs have never left me lethargic like this before. This is Bellamy's fault. Another reason to hate the guy.

I get my espresso machine going and reach for my phone. There are at least a dozen messages waiting for me, as usual, but one of them jumps out at me. It's like I've conjured him up with merely a thought. That's what I get for masturbating to memories of him. This, too, is his fault. Everything is his fault. Ugh.

He's DM'ed me a comment on a shot taken at a photo shoot a while back. It's of me in the shower, back and ass showing through a reflection in the mirror.

@THEBELLAMYBLAIS

Nice shower pic.

What the fuck is that supposed to mean? I stare at those three words, trying to suss out an ulterior motive that might be lurking between the lines. There has to be one. Bellamy doesn't do anything just for the heck of it. He's planning something. He's taunting me, teasing me, trying to coax some sort of reaction out of me. Well, he's going to be sorely disappointed this time.

@OFFICIALLYCARRINGTON

Fuck off.

@THEBELLAMYBLAIS

Damn. Chill.

I should stop. I should ignore him. I should delete the whole message and pretend it never happened.

*Like I'm trying to pretend that Vegas never happened? How's that going?*

I growl at myself.

@OFFICIALLYCARRINGTON

What do you want?

@THEBELLAMYBLAIS

*smirk emoji*

The absolute dick-faced fucker. I toss my phone on the counter and throw back the mini-cup of espresso like it's a shot. The potent dark brew hits me hard, scorching my esophagus as it goes down and spiking my caffeine levels upon contact with my stomach.

Enough of Bellamy Blais. I've got places to be, people to see. I leave the cup in the sink and quickly get dressed in my standard brunch uniform of black jeans, black t-shirt, and black leather jacket. A pair of reflective aviators over my eyes to complete the look.

Then I'm out the door and down to the street to catch my rideshare, my mind not once wandering in Bellamy's direction again. Okay, maybe just once. Or twice. It's not my fault that when I unlock my phone in the car, it's still open to our message thread. My thumb tapping on his name was a legitimate slip of the finger. But since I'm already on his feed, I might as well do some reconnaissance, right?

A shirtless picture on the beach. Another shirtless picture on the beach, the sun setting behind him. Shirtless picture, by a pool this time. Some group shots from Vegas. Promo posts for his edging video. Yet more shirtless pictures next to some type of water. I can't tell if he's a stickler for branding or if he can't afford to buy shirts. Either way, his fans eat it up. Tens of thousands of likes on each post. More than a hundred comments on each too. His follower count is pushing a million and I preen—not as many as me.

The car drops me off in front of the restaurant. I'm the last to arrive. Sebastian, Rhys, and Hayden are already making a dent in their mimosas and they turn in my direction when I drop into my seat.

"What's wrong with you? You look more sour than usual." Sebastian reaches over and gives me a poke like he's testing to see if I'm alive.

I push his hand away. "I'm fine."

They all exchange a look that says they don't believe me.

"Whatever." I wave down a waiter to ask for my own mimosa and we all place our food orders.

"We were just debriefing the Vegas trip," Hayden says, useful as always.

He's the quiet, earnest one in the group. Rhys is the sassy one. Sebastian is our fearless leader and I'm the black sheep.

"Great." I deadpan. Vegas is the last thing I want to talk about.

Across the table from me, Rhys tries to hide his snickers behind his manicured fingers. I glare at him to shut up, but Sebastian and Hayden have already caught on.

"What is it?" Sebastian asks.

"Nothing." I jump in before Rhys can spill whatever juicy piece of gossip he thinks he has. But I've calibrated my tone wrong and it comes out so vehemently that both Sebastian and Hayden swing their gazes back to me.

"Nothing," I say again, more nonchalantly this time. It

doesn't work though, they've caught on to the fact that there is definitely *something*.

"Yeah, uh huh, if 'nothing' also goes by the name Bellamy Blais," Rhys says, gleefully.

"Seriously? Not him again." Sebastian rolls his eyes.

"No, it's not him." A bald-faced lie.

"It totally is." Rhys ignores the death stare I cast his way. "Every time I turned around, there you were, staring into Bellamy's face." He cushions both hands under his chin and gazes off into the distance with big, dreamy eyes.

Seeing that expression on Rhys makes heat rise in me. It creeps up the back of my neck, a hideous mix of anger and embarrassment. I plant my elbow on the table and jab my finger at him. "That is not what I was doing. That is not what I looked like. And besides, his face was all over the fucking place. There was no way to avoid it."

Rhys isn't the least bit fazed. He smiles sweetly back at me like I'm a harmless, snarling puppy. Jerk.

"Oh, and there was the nightclub," Hayden adds. "You know, when Noel disappeared right after Bellamy did?"

I pivot my glare to Hayden. He, for one, reacts the way he's supposed to. His eyes widen as he startles, and he mouths a silent "sorry."

"That's right! You did! What was that about?" Rhys asks, leaning forward, resting his chin in his palm, elbow on the table, like he's waiting for me to tell him a bedtime story.

Images flash across my mind like a montage. Bellamy, leaning against the door frame, head tilted, eyebrow raised, like he was wondering what had taken me so long. The uncontrollable need that came over me, that only ratcheted up when I finally got to taste his mouth. The weight of him on top of me. The glide of his cock against mine.

The table's gone silent while I've been hauled back through time to relive the encounter yet again. When I manage to blink the memories away, I've got three pairs of eyes watching me with curiosity and confusion.

"I already told you. There's nothing going on other than, you know, the usual. He's an asshole and he'll always be an asshole."

Sebastian shakes his head. "You really need to let that go. It's using up way too many brain cells—yours *and* mine. It's not worth it."

The waiter comes back with my mimosa. I take the drink from him and down it all in one go. "Can we just drop it?"

"You know, I've met him once. Bellamy, I mean." Hayden obviously doesn't know the definition of drop it.

Rhys gasps melodramatically, hand on his chest. "Traitor! How can you betray Noel like that?"

I give Rhys a dead-eyed stare. The rivalry is between me and Bellamy and I never asked my friends to choose sides. He doesn't have to go and blow it all out of proportion. But a part of me does delight in his defense—a little loyalty isn't too much to ask.

"He's actually really nice," Hayden says as he pulls out his phone. "He follows me and he's always leaving nice comments."

"Yeah, I bet," I mutter under my breath. The rest of them don't hear me. They're too busy taking pictures of their food and of each other to notice. I check my own phone and sure enough, there's another "nice comment" waiting for me.

@THEBELLAMYBLAIS

Dude, how many purses do you have?

I reach for the handbag sitting on the floor next to me. Then I remember the picture I posted last week—or was it a couple weeks ago—when I was shopping along 5th Avenue.

@OFFICIALLYCARRINGTON

Why do you care? Stalking me?

@THEBELLAMYBLAIS

What do you even carry in them?

Wouldn't you like to know. *eggplant emoji* *droplets emoji*

I smirk at my phone, imagining Bellamy's reaction. Knowing him, he'll probably believe it.

"What are you smiling about?" Sebastian asks, eyes narrowed at me.

I swipe away from Bellamy's DMs and place my phone face down on the table. "Nothing. Can we eat yet? I'm starving."

I shovel a forkful of salad into my mouth, but that doesn't stop the three of them from asking me questions I don't want to answer.

"Is it Bellamy? It's something to do with Bellamy, isn't it?" Rhys is getting way too much entertainment out of this whole thing.

I ignore him and keep chewing.

"You only ever get that look when it has something to do with Bellamy," Rhys continues.

Hayden nods. "You are pretty obsessed with the guy."

"I'm not obsessed," I protest.

They all shake their heads and roll their eyes and finally—*finally*—move on. They don't believe me. That's fine. I don't need them to. The problem is… I'm not sure I believe myself.

## CHAPTER
# EIGHT

## BELLAMY

I'm almost finished my morning run when my phone rings. I tap on my earbuds to answer it.

"Hey, Mom."

"Good morning, dear. I didn't wake you up, did I?"

We're a whole family of early risers, though I suppose they've got a few hours on me over in Cleveland. "Nope, I was just out for a run."

"Oh, do you want to call me back when you're finished?"

"No, I'm good. What's up? How's dad?"

She goes silent for a moment, but I can tell she's stifling a sigh. It's always been like this with her. She thinks she's so good at hiding how bad things are when in reality, I can hear everything in what she leaves unsaid.

"He's... okay."

The pause between the two words is too long for him to actually be okay. "What's wrong? Did something happen?" I stop to check for oncoming traffic before jaywalking across the street to the park. I'm not far from my apartment, but this isn't a conversation I want to have while cooped up in there. I need space to walk it out.

"Nothing's happened. He's fine—"

Whatever else she might have said is cut off by a bout of coughing, thick and phlegmy, from her end of the line. It's my dad, hacking away, and wheezing in between. It sounds worse than usual, but perhaps that's because of my anxiety filter that slotted into place when Mom hesitated.

"He doesn't sound fine, Mom."

She doesn't stifle her sigh this time, and it's accompanied by a door closing, cutting out the background noise.

"He's as fine as he usually is, dear."

"Are you sure?" I fall into a long circuit around the edge of the park, head down, watching the grass squish under my shoes. "He's not getting worse?"

"Well… we all know he's not getting better."

It's my turn to sigh now, and I tilt my head back to gaze up at the sky. It's blue with wisps of white clouds. My feet kick up that morning dew scent and there's still a slight chill in the air.

My dad's poor health is nothing new. We've been dealing with it since I was in high school when his sick leave turned into early retirement. Decades of long-haul truck driving and chain-smoking to idle the hours away inevitably led to a severe case of emphysema in my sophomore year, and then lung cancer not long after. Although he's technically in remission, that doesn't stop his body from trying to expel his lungs every other minute.

"His doctors have switched out a couple meds, though. We're hoping that will help."

I bite back the question on the tip of my tongue. *How*

*much do these new meds costs?* Because even with Medicaid and retirement funds, I'm still making up the bulk of the month-to-month shortfalls in the family finances. Not to mention the mortgage my parents still have on the house.

It's fine, I tell myself. However much it is, I can handle it. Especially since the edging video is doing so well. Maybe they'll ask me to do another one. Or I'll find a product sponsorship somewhere. If we need more money, then I'll make more money. It's *fine.*

"Oh, Twyla's got good news!"

I perk up at the mention of my baby sister. Well, not so baby anymore now that she's a junior.

"Her volleyball team made it to the finals. Her coach said that if she plays well, she might be able to get scholarships for college."

A grin blossoms on my face as I swell with pride, even if it's tinged with a pang of melancholy. I never went to college. It was debatable whether I had the grades to get in, but I didn't even try. We were hanging on by a thread by then and any hour I wasn't physically in school was spent working whatever odd job I could get my hands on. Even if I was accepted into college, there was no way in hell we could've afforded it.

Two weeks after high school graduation, I packed my bags and hitched a ride out to San Francisco with a buddy who promised there was a job waiting for me. There wasn't. But by then I'd already started camming and there was no looking back.

"That's awesome!" I'm really, truly happy for her. She deserves to go to college, to have all the opportunities that a college degree will open up for her. It means I'll have to work more, work harder, but I'll do absolutely everything in my power to make sure finances won't hold her back. "I'll send her a message too, but tell her congratulations for me."

"I will, dear. And, how are you?"

"I'm okay." It's a cop-out answer, about as helpful as her claiming that Dad is fine. But I'm never sure just how much she wants to know about my life.

"Are you staying safe?"

I chuckle under my breath at her concern. Not that it's funny, but more that she's so far removed from the realities of my work that nothing I say will make any sense to her. "Yes, I'm staying safe."

My parents have never been thrilled by the source of my income, but they've never tried to dissuade me from doing what I need to do. Once, about a year ago, Mom even ventured to ask what safety precautions I took—you know, health-wise. I don't know whether the question had been prompted by curiosity or concern, because the second she finished asking, she shook her head and told me not to answer. I didn't press the issue. I can't think of anything worse than explaining PrEP and STI testing to my mom.

"You're not working too hard, are you?"

"No, I'm not working too hard." Especially given that "too hard" is relative. How much is too much when there are bills that need to be paid?

"I don't ever want you to put yourself in danger, dear."

"I know, Mom." *Just don't watch me get tied up and edged.* Not that she ever would. God, that would be bad.

"Just as long as you're being careful."

"I am, Mom."

"Okay, good."

After we hang up, I flop down on the ground and fling an arm over my eyes. I love my family. I do. With my entire being. And the fact that they've accepted my being gay and doing gay porn without all that much fuss is a lot more than others have enjoyed. But every once in a while, when it all feels like too much, when it feels like it's me against life, I wonder what it would be like if things were different.

What if Dad hadn't been a decades-long chain smoker? What if I'd been able to go to college? Where would I be now? What would I be doing? Probably not porn.

I sit up and shake my head. What's the point in dwelling on "what ifs"? Things are the way they are and nothing's going to change them, not unless I get up off my ass and make them change. I push myself to my feet and head back to the apartment I share with Santino.

He's in the kitchen when I get home, wearing nothing but boxer briefs, waiting for the coffee to percolate.

"Hey," he mumbles with a nod.

If I'm a morning person, he's a night owl. It's unusual for him to be awake at this time of day.

"What are you doing up?" I ask, reaching for a mug so I'm ready when the coffee's done.

"Nephew's birthday party today. Gotta go help set up." Santino's got a big family down in Santa Cruz and he makes the trip at least a few times a month.

"Fun. How old is he?"

"Three. He won't have a clue what's going on. It's just an excuse for the rest of us to stuff our faces."

The coffee machine beeps and I pour each of us a cup. Santino takes his and heads back to his room.

"Have a good time at the party," I call out and he raises

his mug in salute.

With the phone call still on my mind, I open my laptop and log into my bank account. There's been a deposit, a nice fat one—royalties from the edging video. Seeing the number on the screen helps settle some of the nerves scratching at the back of my mind. A few more like this one and we should be in the clear for a while.

In my inbox is an email from Fetish Studios. They're co-hosting a kink party in New York and would I like to be a part of the live demonstration? All expenses for the trip would be covered, of course, and there's a hefty paycheck on top of it. Would I? For a paycheck like that, hell yeah, I would.

*You know what else is in New York? Noel Carrington.*

I snort before taking a big gulp of coffee, reveling in the bitter, hot brew. It reminds me of Noel—all sharp and acrid, and yet there's something warm and comforting underneath all the bluster. I have no actual proof of this supposedly warm and comforting inside, but I'm almost positive it's there. No one can be that grumpy on the outside without a soft, marshmallow-y core, right?

*Oh, Noel.*

I pull up his social media and a bubbly thrill rushes through me when I find a new DM waiting for me. I sent that first message after Vegas on a whim, with the memory of our secret rendezvous still lingering on my skin. I wanted to see if we still had our snarky, caustic banter, or if having sex had somehow neutralized the sparks that flew between us over the internet. There'd been nothing to worry about. And now, not only do I get to poke at him in public, I can poke at him in private too! Winning all around.

Noel's comment is on a picture from last summer when I got a nasty sunburn across my shoulders. Interesting. He's been going back through my feed—that's the only way he would've come across a picture so old.

@OFFICIALLYCARRINGTON

Huh, I thought all that orange was from a spray tan.

I snicker and smile gleefully to myself as my thumbs fly over my screen.

@THEBELLAMYBLAIS

You're jealous you didn't get to frolic on the beach with me.

Noel's response comes back rather quickly, which is so goddamn gratifying. A few days ago, he was making me wait at least thirty minutes between messages like he didn't want to look too eager. Guess he's finally given up that pretense.

@OFFICIALLYCARRINGTON

I'd rather roast in hell.

My snicker bursts into a laugh. I can't help it. The grumpier he gets, the more appealing he is. Like some toddler stomping around, not realizing how cute that can be.

"What's so funny?" Santino asks, dressed and looking a lot more alive than when I saw him earlier.

"Noel Carrington."

"That guy? You guys still doing your thing?"

"Yeah." Though it feels different now than it had before Vegas. The public rivalry and the heckling are fun. It's entertaining, a spectacle to see how Noel will react to what I say. Now, there's an additional endearing quality to it. Every rude and scathing comment is cushioned by the knowledge that I had Noel's tongue in my mouth and his cock in my hand. Not that the sniping ever really hurt me, but now, they've almost turned into hugs of a sort. It's weird, I know. It doesn't totally make sense, but then, what about me and Noel has ever totally made sense?

"Why do you hate each other so much anyway?" Santino asks.

"*I* don't hate him." I pause and roll an idea around in my head. Noel certainly acts the part, but the more I interact with him, the less I believe it. "I don't think he hates me either."

Santino shoots me a skeptical look. "Are you sure?"

I shrug. I'm not sure, and if Santino knew about Vegas, he wouldn't be either. But I'm not about to tell him. There's something sacred about that night, a one-off aberration that's never going to happen again. I want to hold it close to me and hog it like a kid who doesn't want to share his favorite toy.

"Whatever," Santino says when I don't have a better answer for him. "I'm out. See you later."

I finish my coffee and go take a shower. By the time I get back to my laptop, I've got the details for the kink party in New York.

*Should I tell Noel that I'm going to be in town?*

I scoff and shake my head. Where the hell did that thought come from? We're not friends. We're not even fuck buddies. Noel won't care if I'm in town or if I'm on his freaking doorstep. If we're lucky, I can get in and out of New York and he'll be non-the-wiser.

# CHAPTER
# NINE

## NOEL

"Tell me again why we're here?" I ask Sebastian as the bouncer lets us past a heavy velvet curtain into the kink club.

I've been here once or twice before, but it's not really my scene. It's not really Sebastian's either, since he's all about the wholesome boy next door vibe.

"We got an invitation," he says with a shrug.

"So?" Technically, *I* got an invitation and I was more than happy to decline it. But once Sebastian found out about the kink party, he insisted that we attend.

"So, I thought we'd come and scope out the competition."

I throw him a skeptical look. None of the people here could even remotely be considered our competition—we're in completely different niches. But he isn't paying attention to me. He's got his eyes peeled for god knows what and probably making a mental list of industry people he wants to network with. Classic Sebastian, always looking for a way to give himself more work.

To be honest, I'm a little dubious about this whole thing. The party's hosted by Fetish Studios, the kink people Bellamy worked with. That doesn't mean he'll be here, obviously, but it doesn't mean he *won't* be here. And even the mere possibility of being in the same building as him has my traitorous eyes trying to pick a certain blond head out of the crowd.

The thing is, I've never worked with any of these people before. They have no reason to want me here other than to stage a run-in with Bellamy. So it's not entirely unfounded for me to have my hackles up, waiting for the guy to pop out from around a corner to jump-scare me.

It wouldn't be hard to do, either. The club is underground with dim lighting and blood-red walls. All the furniture is black vinyl or darkly stained wood. Most of the party is mingling in the main room where a stage holds place of honor at one end, though there are several smaller rooms branching out from it, each with a variety of kinky implements for members' use. The bar is open and since the whole club's been bought out for this party, they're freely serving alcohol. Thank god.

I grab a whiskey for myself and a margarita for Sebastian. He's already talking to someone and when I hand him his drink, he barely even blinks at me. It's fine. I have no interest in whatever their conversation is about. I wander, but as I circle the room, I'm not as inconspicuous as I'd like to think. People are sneaking glances at me, then whispering to each other with these unsettling smiles. They know something I don't. Something's happening that I haven't been made aware of. I don't like it.

I'm about to interrupt Sebastian and suggest we get the hell out of here when the already dim lights cut out completely. The only thing anyone can see is the stage and the studio executive standing there, smarmy and more than a little creepy.

"Thank you all for joining us this evening. I'm sure you're all very excited for our special Shibari demonstration tonight, and especially for our surprise celebrity guest!"

My stomach sinks at the word "surprise." Nothing good ever comes from surprises and if the looks people are throwing in my direction are any indication, I know who the surprise is going to be.

"Did you know about this?" I whisper to Sebastian.

He glances at me in confusion. "About the surprise guest? Yeah, it was on the invitation."

Which doesn't help if I didn't read the thing.

"Do you think it's…?"

I glower instead of answering him.

"Our resident Shibari expert, Rock Seaman, is here to help us celebrate the tenth anniversary of our studio, and here to be all tied up is the one, the only, Bellamy Blais!"

Fuck.

A ripple of applause rolls through the assembled crowd and all eyes turn to me. They want to see my reaction. They want to play us off each other. They think I'm going to make a scene and give them more to gossip about in the next couple days.

Sebastian nudges me with his elbow. "You okay? Want to leave?"

"Can't leave now," I mutter to him, jaw clenched so tight I might crack a molar. There's no discreet way of slipping out anymore, not when there's practically a spotlight on me. And there's no way I'm going to give them the fodder they're all clambering for.

Music pours through the club's speakers as Rock Seaman comes out on stage. Lo-fi beats hum through the air, tingling over my skin, and goosebumps break out across my arms.

Bellamy follows Rock out, wearing a short, black, silk robe. They confer quietly, heads bowed together, Rock's hands resting possessively on Bellamy's shoulders. Something stirs inside me, that undefinable feeling that should be anger but looks suspiciously like lust.

Rock's hand comes up to Bellamy's neck, wrapping around the back, and Bellamy lifts his head to meet Rock's gaze. They stare at each other for a moment, neither of their lips moving, forging some sort of invisible connection that leaves the rest of us on the outside, looking in.

He positions Bellamy center stage, back to us, and slowly strips the robe off Bellamy's shoulders. Underneath, he's wearing nothing but a pair of black briefs, minimal and plain, nothing that will steal attention from the sculpture that is his body.

The lighting is warm on his already bronze skin, highlighting every dip and curve of muscle. The width of his back and the way it tapers to his waist. The long valley of his spine that ends in two dimples right above his ass. That ass—round and firm. My fingers clench around my whiskey glass, wishing it was squeezing something a lot warmer and a lot softer.

Bellamy turns and Rock stands behind him, running hands over Bellamy's chest, arms, hips. Bellamy leans back against him and angles himself to rest their cheeks together. That raging feeling inside me grows, sinking its claws into me, holding me captive. I want to storm out, but I can't. I want to look away, but my eyes are glued to the scene in front of me.

Rock pushes Bellamy to his knees, facing the audience, arms behind his back. The ropes come out, bright red and glowing against the tan of Bellamy's skin. They go around his chest and over his shoulders in a complicated, intricate pattern, and through it all, Bellamy gazes softly at the back of the room. The entire audience is rapt. There isn't a single whisper or shuffle of shoes or shifting of fabric against leather seats.

When Rock leaves him for a moment to reach for a new length of rope, Bellamy sways left and right, his eyes drifting shut, the corners of his mouth tilting up like he's smiling inside. Even when getting tied up, the fucker still looks like he's basking in sunshine.

The new rope gets attached to the web across Bellamy's back, then looped through a ring dangling from the ceiling. Rock tugs on the rope, slowly helping Bellamy to his feet, then off his feet and onto his toes. He holds Bellamy to him, murmuring quietly in his ear until Bellamy settles into that precarious position.

I can barely breathe. My lungs are seized up in this seething feeling that's got me in its grasp. They're so fucking cozy together, whispering and smiling at each other, with Rock's hands all over Bellamy's body. My palms tingle at the memory of touching him. The smoothness of his skin, the slight give in his taut muscles. My dick twitches at the memory of that night too, and at the velvety hardness of his cock.

Rock runs his hand down Bellamy's left leg and wraps

his fingers around the ankle. He lifts it, bending Bellamy's leg and securing it with a ladder of rope running up his thigh. Bellamy's balanced on two toes now, most of his weight held up by the web suspending him from the ceiling. The ropes dig into his flesh as he breathes against them. I follow his quick, shallow rhythm, inhaling when he inhales, exhaling when he exhales. My heart rate rises and my pulse thrums louder and louder until it's blocking out the music. All I know is Bellamy on that stage, bound up in rope, looking like he's seconds away from nirvana.

How dare he? How dare he stand up there, looking the way he does? How dare he make me feel all these things I don't understand and don't want to feel? He's taken over everything, caught me in his net, I can't fucking step outside my own home without running into him. I can't pick up my damn phone without seeing his face on the screen.

Rock is on his knees, tying yet another length of rope around Bellamy's right ankle. He runs the rope through his hand and feeds the end around the ring holding Bellamy off the floor. When he tugs, Bellamy's leg arcs back in a curve graceful enough for a ballerina. He gives Bellamy's shoulder a nudge, and suddenly he's spinning, suspended in midair. A collective gasp shoots across the audience at the sight of Bellamy all trussed up and on display.

A couple spins later, Rock gently brings him to a stop. Bellamy lifts his head, opens his eyes… and looks directly into mine.

It's possible he doesn't see me. He's so deep in whatever headspace Rock's got him in that I might be nothing but a dark blur against a darker background. But his gaze doesn't waver and his lips part, pursing just enough that it looks like he could be silently mouthing my name. It sets me back on my heels and almost brings me to my knees.

I want to take his face in my hands and run my lips over every inch of it. I want to spin him around, drawing my palms over the bulges of flesh framed by unyielding red rope. I want to unzip my pants, take out my cock, and feed it to him as he's hanging helplessly from the ceiling. Fuck, I want him. So much that my dick throbs in my pants and heat pools in my joints.

I'm one second away from making a huge fucking mistake by striding up onto the stage when Rock steps in front of Bellamy, severing this mysterious link between us. We're not entirely disconnected though. I can still feel him like a ghost over my skin, like a weight against my body. He's there. He's always fucking there. I can't escape him.

Rock starts unraveling Bellamy, moving in reverse order, lowering first the right leg, then the left. It takes just as long, but now that the ta-da moment is over, the crowd is stirring again. And the first thing they latch onto is me.

Inquiring minds try to assess my reaction to what we witnessed on the stage. Did I like it? Did I hate it? Am I going to say something to them? Am I going to post anything online? Jokes on them, because I'm not doing any of that.

I toss back whatever's left of my whiskey and set the glass down on the nearest flat surface. Sebastian's waiting for a signal from me and at my nod, he turns toward the exit. I follow him out, my back on fire from all those eyes boring into it.

"That was…" Sebastian trails off when we make it out onto the street.

I don't take his bait. I have nothing to say about Bellamy Blais, not to the people still inside the club, and not to him.

"You all right?"

"Fine," I say. I take a breath and let it out in fits and starts. There's a trembling unsteadiness in me, like a line pulled so tight that it starts vibrating right before it snaps.

Sebastian knows me well enough to leave me to my stewing. His rideshare arrives first and I say goodbye with a promise to check in tomorrow. When my car finally shows up, I carefully fold myself into the backseat, feeling fragile and on edge. Any little jostle could set me right off.

My hands tingle as I pull up our DM thread. No heads-up that he was going to be in town. No mention of it either on any of his social media feeds. His appearance was supposed to be a surprise after all. Surprise or not, he's not leaving until I get some answers.

He can't come traipsing through my city, string me along like that, and then disappear across the country again. He owes me for stoking up this fury that I can barely control. And I'm going to make him pay.

# CHAPTER
# TEN

## BELLAMY

It's late when I get to the address on my phone. I'm not even sure I'm supposed to be here. There was no context in the message, just an address timestamped around the time we were finishing up the Shibari demonstration. Noel had marched out of the club by then. I watched him go with a trepidation that chilled my insides.

I didn't know he was going to be there. I mean, of course, there was always a chance that he would be—this is his city, after all. But I didn't ask the studio to invite him and they didn't tell me what they were planning. I was so focused on the demonstration, on staying in the headspace Rock needed me in, that I didn't see any of the faces in the audience. Not until I lifted my head to ease the pressure on my neck, blinked at the rush of blood, and spotted him. Standing against the red wall, all dressed in black, a now-familiar scowl on his face.

He was staring at me so intently, like nothing and no one else in the room existed. Just me and him. Me, all bound up, lightheaded and dazed. Him, a dark presence that sucked in all the light. I wanted to go to him. I wanted him to come to me. I wanted him to wrap his arm around me and let me press my face against his skin the way Rock did when I needed to be grounded.

But we didn't do any of that. Instead, Noel walked out, and it felt like he took something with him—a piece of me.

And now I'm here to get it back. At least that's what I'm telling myself. Why else would I be here?

*Because Noel gave you his address and you can't say no.*

I don't know what I'm expecting to find up there. A shouting match? Sex? Some sort of penance for walking out on me when I was literally tied and bound with no way to chase after him? All I know is I'm missing something, something vital, and Noel's holding it hostage.

A liveried doorman greets me as I enter the towering condo building in East Village.

"You must be Mr. Blais."

That he knows my name takes me aback. "Yes," I say, cautiously. "That's me."

"I've been instructed to send you right up."

Figures that Noel told him to expect me. Presumptuous, but not uncharacteristic.

The doorman ushers me into the elevator and he pokes his head in to press the button for the top floor. "There you go. All the way up. You have a good evening."

Penthouse. Figures. Nothing but the best for Noel Carrington.

The elevator spits me out in a hallway and Noel's unit is at the far end. I only get midway through my knock when the door opens, like Noel had been waiting right next to it. Like he'd been impatient for me to show up. I can't help but smile at the thought—entitled and self-absorbed Noel, waiting for me with bated breath. It's flattering.

He stands in the doorway, staring at me with that intensity I've come to associate with him. Piercing and forceful, its weight is palpable as he trains it on me. It's the same look he had at the club earlier when he watched me like I was the only person in the room and he wanted to take me apart and devour me.

Well, now's his chance. And he leaves me standing out here?

"Are you going to invite me in?" I quirk my lips into a smile that I know will annoy him.

His brows draw together in a scowl and I warm in satisfaction at how easily he's played.

Noel steps back to let me squeeze past him. My shoulder brushes his chest and my muscles twitch at the contact. I'm pretty sure he suppresses a shudder too.

Once I get inside though, holy shit. This place. If I hadn't already guessed Noel was rich from his address alone, this condo confirms it beyond a shadow of a doubt. The windows aren't quite floor-to-ceiling, but they occupy a significant chunk of the wall. The building is tall enough that the lights of lower Manhattan twinkle in front of us like we're hovering above the stars.

Other than the white walls, everything else is dark: dark wood, dark leather, dark trim around the windows. A well-stocked minibar sits along one wall and a huge fireplace sits along another. There isn't a single item out of place. Even the stack of books on the coffee table looks like it's been specifically placed there to be seen and admired. I've just walked onto the set of a home decor photo shoot.

"You live here?" Normally, that'd be a ridiculous question to ask someone who sent me his address. But no one really lives in a place like this. I'm afraid to touch anything in case I smudge up all the shiny surfaces with my fingerprints.

"Yeah." Noel folds his arms over his chest like he's daring me to argue with him. "My parents own a real estate company. This is an investment property."

It all makes sense now. He lives off mommy and daddy's dime, leaving him with plenty of cash to spend at all those luxury brand stores he's constantly posting pictures of. Those handbags he loves so much are pocket-change compared to the money needed for a place like this.

"Right. Cool." No point in telling him that my parents were a truck driver and a kindergarten teacher before they retired. Or that they had to refinance the house to make ends meet.

Noel goes to the minibar. "Want something to drink?" he asks, though he doesn't wait for an answer before pouring two glasses.

"Sure." Whiskey's not usually my drink of choice. I'm more of a "whatever is the cheapest beer available" kind of guy. But when Noel hands me a tumbler and I take a sip, the amber liquor goes down smooth and warm. This is the expensive shit. Why am I not surprised?

Noel takes his and tosses the whole thing back so fast there's no way he tasted any of it. He pours himself another while I take a slow sip of mine.

If I didn't know better, I would say that Noel is nervous. But Noel Carrington doesn't get nervous. Not around some peon like me. So why is he suddenly too shy to look at me? His arms are crossed and he's gripping his glass hard enough that the tips of his fingernails go white. Tension radiates from him like some sort of forcefield and I want to take a run at him to see if I'll bounce off the invisible shield he's erected around himself.

But underneath all that posturing, there's a vulnerability I'm sure he doesn't want me to see. I've noticed traces of it before. In the fitness room in Vegas, right before he ran out. When he came to my hotel room that night. He might not even know it's there—maybe that's why he looks so freaked out when it starts pushing its way to the surface. He's spent so much time pretending to be the too-cool-for-school Noel Carrington that he's not used to being a normal person like the rest of us.

The demonstration at the club must've affected him as much as it affected me. Why else would he send me his address? Why else would he warn his doorman that I was coming? Something passed between us in those few moments when our gazes locked and we both need to close the loop.

"Noel," I say, gently, like I'm trying to calm a terrified stray dog. "Why did you invite me here?" I want him to put it into words. I want to hear him say it out loud.

His frown hardens and his jaw ticks. "Why did you come?"

It's going to be like that, is it? He wants me here, but he doesn't want to want me here. Story of his life, it seems.

"I can leave." I set my glass down on a side table.

"No," Noel snaps as he steps forward. He's vibrating from whatever internal duel he's fighting with himself. His nostrils flare with every breath, his lips are pressed into a thin, straight line. He looks like he's about to burst.

I stand there, waiting and watching, holding as still as I can so I don't startle him into doing something he'll blame me for later. It doesn't take long before he breaks.

"Fuck." He shoves his free hand through his hair and spins on his heel, stalking away from me.

I let out the breath I hadn't realized I was holding and my next inhale nudges me into motion. "Noel."

He flinches at the sound of his own name, but he doesn't move as I approach him. I take that as a good sign. I carefully wrest the glass from his hand and set it down on the side table next to mine.

"Can you look at me?"

It takes him a moment, dark lashes fluttering against his smooth, pale cheeks, before he lifts his gaze. Swirling pools of deepest brown that would look black to anyone who wasn't standing so close. Mahogany, chestnut, and russet, each shade darker than the last, drawing me into their depths.

"Noel." It comes out as a whisper this time, as a plea. That connection from the club, that thing that passed between us, it's right here, close enough to grasp. It's tenuous, fleeting, waiting to see if we're brave enough to seize it.

I want it, though I'm not entirely certain why. There's no reasoning, no logic behind this bone-deep yearning I have. It's not about how attractive Noel is or how he reacts to my merciless teasing. I mean, that's all there, all legitimate, but there's something else luring me closer, something more primal, more instinctual. Like my lizard brain sees something in Noel that it knows is good for me.

I take another step closer, close enough that when Noel sucks in a lungful of air, his chest almost brushes against mine. We always find ourselves like this. Nose-to-nose, toe-to-toe, facing off like we're about to enter into battle. There's an honesty to it that I appreciate. No hiding, no pretending that we're anything other than exactly what we are. We're not friends, not fuck buddies. He can barely stand me and he's not my favorite person either. Despite all that, there's a magnetism between us we can't ignore. It's impossible to resist.

# CHAPTER
# ELEVEN

**NOEL**

Sunshine doesn't have a scent. It should be impossible to smell. So why the hell does Bellamy's proximity immediately make me think of warm rays on my skin, sand between my toes, and the sound of rushing waves in the background?

And the way he said my name. With that hint of desperation and helplessness, like he was as powerless against this thing as I am. This is lunacy, someone's idea of a practical joke, throwing the two of us together, making us want each other.

The rage boiling in me since the club ebbed into anxiety after I got home. I practically wore a path into my hardwood floors while waiting to see if Bellamy would show up.

But then he did. And the anxiety has bubbled back up into anger again. Anger that he didn't tell me he would be in town. That I had to find out the way I did. Anger that I wanted him here in my apartment so badly that I couldn't stop myself from sending him my address.

"You didn't tell me you were in New York." It bothers me. It shouldn't, but it does. He's been in New York dozens of times in the past and I couldn't have cared less. This time is different though.

"I didn't know I was supposed to tell you."

The muscle in my jaw ticks from how hard I'm clenching my teeth.

"Is this your thing now? Getting tied up?" Red rope marks encircle his wrists like cuffs. They probably criss-cross over his chest and arms too. I can still see him back there, all trussed up on the stage. My fingers itch to trace those lines, to dig in and see how tender they are.

Bellamy shrugs. "Maybe. It pays well."

I bet it does. There's a degree of trust involved with kink that us vanilla camboys know nothing about. I wouldn't let anyone tie me up like that, no matter how good they were at it. It suits Bellamy though—I like him better when he's defenseless and vulnerable.

"Simple camming isn't cutting it for you?"

Bellamy's eyes flash, going gray and stormy for a second before clearing again. It's here and gone so fast I might've missed it if I wasn't mere inches away from him. Satisfaction hums through me—so Bellamy can get rattled. He's not quite as unflappable as he makes himself out to be.

He lets out a laugh that sounds more bitter and biting than I thought he was capable of, then takes a step back. A hint of panic spikes through me—where does he think he's going?

"It tears you up inside, doesn't it?" Bellamy takes another step back.

I inch forward, needing to close the distance between us. "What tears me up?"

"Wanting me. You hate that you want me, but you can't stop. The more you try to fight it, the stronger it gets." He backs up again and I follow him.

He's right. We both know it. But I'm not going to let him gloat by admitting to it. I lean into the rumbling anger instead, letting it surge up, fast and uncontrollable. I grab Bellamy with both hands and drag him to me, slamming our mouths together like some fucked up attempt at CPR.

Bellamy's hands come to my hips, jerking me against him. He's hard already and he grinds his erection into mine like we're trying to light kindling on fire. I shove my tongue into his mouth and he sucks it like a lollipop he can't get enough of. He scrapes his teeth along the top, along the bottom, and the sharp drag sends heat rocketing through me.

Fuck. The things he does to me, throwing me off-kilter, turning my world upside down. He's a goddamn invasive species, infiltrating my life and my mind, suffocating everything else until all I can think about—all I can obsess about—is Bellamy, Bellamy, Bellamy.

I shove him away from me so forcefully he stumbles backward. We glare at each other in a contest I'm determined to win and yet I'm certain I'm going to lose. There's no defeating this thing. There's only capitulating and hoping it'll work itself out of my system.

I grab the hem of my shirt and strip it off. Bellamy gets the message, unbuttoning his jeans while kicking off his shoes. It's frantic, clothes flying everywhere, and when we're finally naked, we come crashing back together. Every point of contact lights up like a spark, sending electricity zinging through me until I'm tingling all over. I shiver and shudder under his touch, nipples hardening and cock leaking. My balls draw up and my guiche feels achingly heavy.

We shuffle clumsily in the direction of the couch, not willing to come apart to watch where we're going. Bellamy grunts in surprise when he hits the armrest and tumbles over it. I go after him as he scrambles on his elbows.

My mouth finds his again and our tongues swipe, slide, and push against each other. Greedy. Hungry. Demanding. My thigh is wedged up high between his and his balls are full and fragile where they're pressed against my quad. Bellamy moans and arches up into me.

I kiss across his jaw, up to that dip below his ear, then nibble my way down his neck. My lips find the spot where his heartbeat pulses and when I add my teeth into the mix, Bellamy moans again.

His chest is covered in an intricate pattern of bruised red lines that I trace, first with my fingertips, then my tongue, then my teeth. Bellamy hisses and sighs, growing louder while I work my way across each one. My mouth is saturated with the salty taste of him. My skin tingles as my jaw closes around his flesh, leaving my own marks on top of the ones he already has.

My chin bumps against his cock, hard and heavy and leaking on his stomach. It's long and thick with juicy veins running up and down its length and a perfectly shaped bulbous head that's currently as red as his chest. It's a nice cock—too nice. No one should have a cock so flawless. No wonder Bellamy's so full of himself when he's walking around with this thing between his legs.

I rub my stubbled cheek against it and Bellamy gasps. His hips jerk and when I glance up, he's scowling at me. I grin and do it again.

"Fucker." He's gripping the cushions around him, knuckles going white.

I lick a wide, wet path from the base of his dick all the way up to his tip before wrapping my lips around the glans and wiggling my tongue into his slit.

"Fuck!" Bellamy's hips come straight off the couch and I have to use my entire body to push him back down.

I tease his slit again.

"God, Noel, fuck." He's so vocal during sex.

I thought it was for the cameras when I watched his videos. But there are no cameras here, no one watching us, no one to perform for. And he's still babbling curses in between whines and cries, groans and moans, until it's a cacophony of incoherent sounds.

I take Bellamy all the way to my throat and swallow. He throws his head back to reveal that long column of neck. "Please, Noel, please."

The way he says my name. God. Dripping with lust. Oozing with need. He's desperate and I'm the only one who can do anything about it. I'm the only one who can satisfy him.

I pull off, leaving his cock waving in the air, engorged and covered in spittle. Power swells in me at the sight of him, Bellamy Blais, laid out on my couch like this. Eyes half-lidded and hazy with desire. Skin flushed and coated with a sheen of sweat. Arousal thrumming through him, through his pulsing cock, and the rapid rise and fall of his chest.

*I* did this to him. I, Noel Carrington, have reduced Bellamy Blais to a whimpering, squirming mess. And I'm nowhere near done.

I grab Bellamy's hand and tug him until I've got him where I want him. Knees on the seat, chest resting on the back of the couch, ass perfectly angled for my access. I position myself behind him, hands on those plump round ass cheeks, pulling them apart to reveal his tight pink hole. Bellamy clenches and it looks like the hole is winking at me, daring me to lick it, to pry it open and stretch it wide. I don't need to be challenged twice.

"Oh, fuck!"

Bellamy pushes his ass toward me as my lips seal around his hole. I don't try to warm him up or tease him. He doesn't need any warnings. I simply narrow my tongue to a point and drill it right through the center of his opening. The muscle gives under me, filling my mouth with flavor that shouldn't be possible. It's muskier than the rest of him, darker and more potent, and yet it still tastes like fucking sunshine. Molten hot, with flares bursting from the surface of the sun, lashing me in the face.

"Fuck, Noel! Fuck!"

I slap him, hard enough that my palm stings. It doesn't shut him up though, it only makes his voice go up an octave.

"Jesus Christ, fuck me already!"

A string of pre-cum dangles from the tip of his cock and drops down onto the couch. His toes curl and stretch, curl and stretch, like he's trying to fight off an orgasm.

While I was waiting for him to show up, I tucked some supplies behind a throw pillow. I felt ridiculous at the time, but clearly my subconscious had known something past-me hadn't wanted to acknowledge. We were always going to end up here tonight. Naked, fucking on the couch, driving each other to ruin.

I squirt lube onto my fingers and stab two into Bellamy's ass. The sound coming from him is more a scream than a cry, but he tilts his hips to take my fingers deeper. I find his prostate and jam my fingers into it. He screams again. Another gush of pre-cum lands on my couch.

"Motherfucker," he gasps.

I've never been so proud of a compliment before.

I yank my fingers out and jab them in again, digging at his prostate until Bellamy's sobbing. Only then do I suit myself up and aim my cock at his trembling hole. I take my time sliding into him, savoring the tight heat, the sight of my dick disappearing into his body, the whimpers that are music to my ears.

I have to pause when I bottom out. It so goddamn good to be inside Bellamy. Much too good. It's just an ass, I tell myself. It's no different than any other ass I've fucked. And yet, I'm shaking with something more than simple pleasure.

I'm shaking with triumph. I've conquered. I've subdued. I've taken this enemy and made him mine. Mine to take apart. Mine to wreck.

I fuck him. I fuck him as hard and fast as possible. My fingers clamp around his hips so firmly, he's going to walk away with bruises. That is, if he'll be able to walk at all. He won't if I have anything to do about it.

I drive into him, finding the exact angle to pound on his prostate. Sweat flies off us. The air is soaked through with the scent of man and sex. Bellamy's screaming, his voice hoarse now, and there's a second voice layered on top of his.

It's mine, shouting "fuck" on repeat like it's the only word in my vocabulary.

My guiche swings, tugging at the skin on my perineum. The weighty ring slaps against the back of my balls until they're tender and throbbing. Pressure builds inside me, drawing blood from the far reaches of my body and gathering it all in my groin.

My orgasm hits like a tidal wave racing toward the beach. It crashes into me and sucks me down, churning around me until I don't know which way is up. I can't breathe. The pressure is crushing and the only point of release is through my cock. Wave after wave, it pummels me until I can't stand anymore. I collapse on top of Bellamy, spent and drained, only vaguely aware of his own orgasm as it paints my couch with cum.

# CHAPTER
# TWELVE

## BELLAMY

I follow the marketing assistant to a dressing room at the Los Angeles photography studio. Noel's already sitting in a makeup chair and he looks up when I enter. It takes a millisecond for his expression to coalesce into a scowl when he spots me in the wall of mirrors in front of him.

My body lights up like it's been waiting to be in the same room as Noel again. My skin tingles and my gut clenches at the healthy dose of adrenaline rushing through my veins. A light bubbly feeling grows in my chest. I smirk when I take the seat next to him.

"Mr. Carrington," the marketing assistant clutches her tablet. "We'll be ready for you soon. I'll come get you in a few minutes."

"Mr. Carrington, huh?" I say, quietly, after she leaves.

"Shut up. I told her to call me Noel."

"You're too old and curmudgeonly to be just Noel."

"Fuck you."

Ah, I missed this. It's been a few months since that

night in New York. Since I let myself get tied up and Noel was in the audience watching. Since I went to his apartment and he fucked me over the back of his couch. I had bruises from that fucking. Sitting through the flight home to San Francisco the next day was pure hell. Santino asked if I'd hurt myself while I was gone.

Also, apparently, my cum is corrosive and his precious leather couch is stained beyond repair. I have a hard time believing that, but hey, what the hell do I know about leather couches?

That message from Noel was waiting for me when I landed and since then we've been going back and forth non-stop. Nothing substantial. Nothing important. Just inane things that grade schoolers throw across the playground to insult each other.

Then last week I get a message from Noel.

@OFFICIALLYCARRINGTON

You fucking asshole.

@THEBELLAMYBLAIS

*smirk emoji* What did I do now?

The photo shoot.

For the underwear company? How do you know about that?

It's supposed to be my photo shoot.

I'm pretty sure it's my photo shoot. I've had it scheduled for ages.

So have I.

Turns out, it's both of ours. Monte's Manties hired both

of us as brand reps, and then conveniently neglected to inform us that we'll be doing the photo shoot together. People love pitting us against each other. As underhanded as it is, I have to admit that whoever thought this up is pretty genius.

We've been rivals for a long time. And yet, it feels like the rivalry is getting more intense lately—with Vegas and then the kink party. There were no cell phones allowed in the kink club, but somehow pictures of Noel standing there, watching me, still managed to make it onto the internet. The lust. The hate. The obsession. The fans fucking loved it. It's not a surprise that people want to see more of us together.

The marketing assistant comes back to escort Noel away to do a series of solo shots before I join him. The makeup artist stops in to fix my face and then hands me my outfit for the day. It's a scrap of fabric, at least a size too small for me. But when I put on the jockstrap, I have to admit I look fucking hot. My cock is barely contained in the red fabric with black trim, making me look significantly bigger than I actually am.

Noel's sitting in a plush, upholstered chair when I'm led out, with one leg hiked up over the armrest and his head thrown back. The photographer's standing on a box to get an overhead shot. I can imagine what it looks like. Noel, with his signature smolder, skin glistening, his dick a massive bulge in the thong they've got him in. Black with red trim—my perfect opposite.

From where I'm standing, his legs are spread wide and the fabric of his thong disappears between the globes of his ass cheeks. I'm pretty sure I can see the outline of his piercing and my cock twitches at the memory of it.

I turn away. I'm practically bursting out of this jock-strap already and I don't need a boner in the middle of a photo shoot. The makeup person has me shrug off the bathrobe I'm wearing and proceeds to slather me with baby oil. *That's* why Noel looks so shiny.

When they're all done with me and I turn to face Noel again, I'm struck by the expression on his face. He's staring at me, perusing me. His gaze travels down my body, then all the way back up, warming me despite the air conditioning in the studio. When he makes eye contact, I can't help but smirk. He likes what he sees. He wants me. He's hungry for me.

I'm hungry for him too. I didn't realize how much until I walked into the dressing room and my body came alive. In all our messages, we haven't once brought up sex—the sex we've already had or the sex we might have in the future. But our bodies know something our minds don't, that we feel good when we're together, that we crave each other.

"Bellamy, hi, I'm Parker. Let's get you here next to Noel." The photographer waves me over and I take my mark. "I want to get a series of shots with the two of you standing off. I want to see intensity and fire. You hate each other, but you want to fuck each other at the same time. Can you do that?"

Can we do that? That's the basis of our entire relationship. That's the only way we know how to be.

"Sure thing, Parker," I say to the photographer, though my gaze is locked on Noel.

"All right. Awesome." Parker steps back and brings his camera up to his face. "Get in a little closer, a little more..."

Noel and I shuffle toward each other until our toes

bump together. Instead of backing off though, I push forward, lifting my big toe to pin his to the floor.

His eyes narrow. His jaw ticks. His mouth twists into a snarl.

A grin tugs on my lips and giddy satisfaction ripples through me.

"Yes! That's it! That's what I'm talking about!" Parker shouts encouragement from behind his camera. "You two are naturals!"

Does he not know about our rivalry? Did he think we'd have to *act* for this? No, dude. We were made for this —*born* for this.

Noel yanks his toe out and pins my toe in return. I wiggle it, trying to burrow deeper under his foot. His eyes grow darker, harder, the browns swirling with anger and heat. I bite back a snicker even as my cock twitches from the intensity of Noel's stare.

"Love it! Amazing! Lean in a bit closer. Almost like you're going to kiss."

Any closer and we *are* going to kiss. Kiss or shove each other. Noel's practically vibrating from having to hold himself back. His breathing is getting heavier, every exhale a burst of warm air across my cheek.

His gaze drops to my mouth and my cock perks up at the possibility of getting some action. No matter that we're in public, with a camera trained at us. It only cares about rubbing up on Noel's body, maybe getting inside it.

Fuck. I can imagine it already. Noel spread out on a bed, fingers clutching at the sheets. The wild look in his eyes as he fights himself. Every muscle tense, bracing for the pleasure he knows will overwhelm him. The way he'll come apart when I sink into him.

"Perfect! Utterly perfect!" Parker hands off his camera to an assistant and points to a purple velvet chaise sitting off to the side. "Let's switch things up."

It takes a lot of effort to step back from Noel. To keep my hands to myself rather than grab him and crush our mouths together. My heart slams against my chest. The sweat breaking out at my temples and along the back of my neck have nothing to do with the heat of the studio lights trained on us. The makeup person rushes over with tissues to dab me until I'm camera-ready again.

The chaise is set up in the middle of a white backdrop and Noel is glaring at it in disgust as if it's the ugliest piece of furniture he's ever laid eyes upon.

"We're going for a wrestling feel, okay?"

Noel's head snaps around so fast I'm surprised he doesn't get whiplash. "What?"

Parker doesn't notice the venom in Noel's voice. "You know, wrestling. Noel, you're sort of half kneeling on the couch thing. Bellamy, you're behind him, trying to restrain him or something. And Noel, you're going to resist or try to throw him off."

Noel's scowl grows deeper with every word coming out of Parker's mouth and when I can't contain myself anymore, I burst out laughing. Parker glances at me quizzically. "Is something funny?"

"No, nothing. Sorry." I flash him a smile. "Wrestling. Got it."

Parker leaves us to retrieve his camera.

"This is bullshit," Noel mutters under his breath.

"It's a job."

"A bullshit job."

"Suck it up, princess." I step behind him and put my hands on his shoulders to guide him toward the chaise.

He shrugs me off with a dirty look thrown over his shoulder. "Fuck you."

"That's the vibe!" Parker waves at the chaise. "But on the couch thing!"

Noel sets one knee on the seat of the chaise, the other foot still planted on the floor. I sidle up close and put my hands on him again. He tenses under my touch but otherwise doesn't object. I slide one arm around his chest and pull him flush to me. A shudder runs through him—through us.

Parker's on the floor, practically lying down, taking shots at us from below. I angle myself so I'm offset from Noel. The camera can't see the merchandise if I grind my erection into Noel's ass like I want to.

Noel twists, and all greased up like we are, he slips out of my grasp. I grab him again, forcefully enough that we pitch forward. Noel catches us, hands on the chaise, with me flattened against his back.

"Yes, good. Keep going. More of that."

He shoves his elbow in my direction and it kind of feels like he's fighting for real because it lands in my side harder than I expect. "Fucker," I gasp into his ear. He huffs in satisfaction.

I lick his face. Flat of my tongue, thick straight stripe from his jaw to his temple, slow enough that I know Parker got plenty of shots of it.

"Ew, gross. Asshole!" Noel dislodges me and I go tumbling onto the chaise. He rounds on me, murder in his eyes. "What the fuck?"

"Wait! Wait! Hold that!" Parker scrambles to his feet,

waving at his assistant to reposition some of the reflective panels.

Noel looks like he wants to strangle me and my face is split into a grin so big my cheeks are starting to ache.

"Okay, I'm good. Go!"

Noel throws a scowl at Parker, clearly unimpressed at having a camera still trained on us. I adjust so I'm sprawled out, arms draped across the back cushions, legs spread, cock and jockstrap on display. I dare Noel to come at me, to do his worst.

He does. But not the way I expect.

He wraps his hand around my ankle and yanks, dragging me forward so I'm lying on my back. The move knocks the wind out of me, leaving me defenseless when Noel launches himself. He presses his forearm against the base of my throat. Forcefully enough that I know he means it, but not quite enough to leave bruises. He snarls right into my face.

I grab his hips and jerk him down. A spike of pleasure surges through me when his erection collides with mine. He reaches for my wrist, but I get my fingers around the thin strap of his thong and tug.

"Fuck!" Noel throws his head back. The fabric between his ass cheeks rubs on his hole. I know because his cock jerks against mine.

We wrestle. Slick skin and grabby hands and muttered curses. I give up trying to maintain a good angle for the camera. Parker can work around us. Somehow, we end up with Noel under me, face down on the chaise. I've got my hand on the back of his neck and I'm sitting on his thighs to keep him from kicking me in the balls.

"Yes! This is fucking fantastic! Bellamy, bend down, like you're whispering threats into Noel's ear."

I push my fingers into Noel's hair and grab a handful to pull his head back, exposing the length of his neck. Leaning down, my lips brush against the shell of his ear. "You like this, don't you? I can tell." From the flush of his skin, the speed of his breaths, and the erection that's currently hidden under him. From the way he shudders at my words and how his Adam's apple bobs when he swallows.

"Fuck you, asshole."

I smile, wicked and sinful. "No, I think next time I'll be fucking you." I tilt my hips and grind my cock into Noel's ass. He rewards me with another shudder and I lick into his ear.

# CHAPTER
# THIRTEEN

## NOEL

"Fuck! Jesus! What is wrong with you?" Either Bellamy is in a licking mood today, or he's got a fetish I don't know about. I have a face full of makeup and he just goes and slathers his tongue all over my cheek. And now he's giving me a fucking wet willy.

I struggle against him, but he's got me pinned somehow, with my left arm stuck uselessly under me. The right one though… I reach back and make contact with Bellamy's leg, then I drag my hand up to his inner thigh, as high as I can go, and I pinch. Hard.

"Ow! Fuck!" He jumps and that's all the space I need to shove him the rest of the way off me. He sits back on his ass, rubbing at the mark I left on him and glowering at me with a pout.

A thrill of gratification settles my indignant, rioting anger. But it only lasts for a minute, for as long as it takes for the traitorous part of me to want to fucking soothe him. To kiss his goddamn booboo and maybe distract him from the pain with a blowjob. My mouth is suddenly watering. Christ.

I'm a fucking mess when it comes to Bellamy. My reactions are all over the place, rage-y one moment and tender the next. And the more we interact, the more confused my psyche seems to get.

I was pissed when I found out we'd be doing this shoot together. It wouldn't have been difficult to hire a lawyer and get out of the contract. But I didn't, because underneath the annoyance and anger was something else.

Excitement. Anticipation. An uncomfortable awareness that I knew exactly how many days it'd been since we'd last seen each other. An even more unsettling realization that I was counting down the days until we'd see each other again.

There is something wrong with me. There has to be. I. Don't. Like. The. Guy. And yet, I'd been looking forward to this day with way too much enthusiasm, way too much eagerness.

It took a Herculean amount of self-control for me not to jump Bellamy the second he took off that goddamn bathrobe, leaving him in nothing but a jockstrap. And when they put the baby oil on him. Holy hell. The seething lust I have for him threatened to consume me whole. I needed to get my hands on him, if not right that fucking second, then soon.

Parker and his ridiculous wrestling have only made it worse. The slick slide of Bellamy's body against mine, the heat of him against me, the possessive way he's touching me, groping me, holding me.

We move out of the studio next, to a deserted hallway on the building's upper floor. There's a skylight in the ceiling and sunlight spills in through the glass, turning the hallway into a glowing, almost ethereal space.

I get to pin Bellamy this time. With his back against the wall and arms raised above his head. I hold his wrists with one hand and his jaw with the other. A wild part of me wants to spit in his mouth. The idea shocks me as much as it turns me on and I grip him harder to try to rein myself in.

Bellamy's lips twitch like he's about to break out into a grin. Like he thinks this is all so funny, a great big joke. And to him, it probably is. I bet the guy hasn't taken a single thing seriously in his whole life. But the feelings he brings out in me, the way he gets me all mixed up, it's not a joke to me. I hate that he has this effect on me. I hate that I react to him so strongly, so viscerally.

"All right, Noel. Go ahead and feel him up," Parker calls to us from behind the camera.

I slowly slide my hand down and wrap my fingers around Bellamy's throat. He lifts his chin like he's giving me more access. His eyes flash when I tighten my hold, not enough to cut off his air supply, but enough to make it feel like a threat. Then the icy blues of his irises turn a little muddled and gray. He takes a long, deep breath and I can feel the air rushing through his windpipe. My fingers are on his quickening pulse.

I drag my hand lower, to his chest and a nipple. He gasps when I pinch it and swallows down a moan when I twist it. When I glance down his body, I think I can see a wet spot forming on the fabric of his jockstrap. I smirk. That's going to go over real well in the photos.

With my palm against his body, fingers pointed down, I venture lower, over his ribs and the flat of his stomach.

My fingertips brush up against the waistband of the jockstrap.

Bellamy's not smiling now. He's not smirking or defiant or smug. He's shaking. Brows furrowed, breath coming hard and fast. His hips come off the wall, searching for something to rub his cock on, but I push him back.

Next to us, Parker's on his knees, camera lens pointed low for a close-up shot. We're both hard, stretching the fabric of our underwear to the limit. There's less than an inch between my erection and his. It almost feels like our dicks are straining for each other, desperate to get reacquainted. My hand is covering Bellamy's hip, my fingers tucked under the elastic of his jockstrap and poking out the other side.

"Shit." Parker lowers his camera and looks up at us. "You two are super hot, you know that?"

Oh yeah, we know. Even when we don't want to.

Parker stands. This part of the shoot is over, but I don't step back, I don't take my hands off Bellamy. As much as I hate admitting it, it feels good to touch him and my body isn't ready to let go.

Bellamy's lips part. It would be easy to lean in and crush our mouths together, to bite down on that plump bottom lip and have him whimper underneath me. My hand inches sideways from his hip inward to his crotch. His stomach muscles contract at the movement.

"Noel, you're all done!"

I jerk backward so fast I nearly take Bellamy's jockstrap with me. His hand flies to where mine was a second ago, like he's trying to keep the heat of my palm on his skin.

I tear my gaze away from him. Parker and his assistant

are already at the end of the hallway and I march toward them. I can't believe how close I was to kissing Bellamy just now. It didn't matter that we had an audience, that there was a camera trained right at us. The craving for him, for a taste of him was staggering. It still is, thrumming through my veins and tempting me to turn around and haul him to me.

If Parker hadn't called out my name... god, I don't want to contemplate what I would've done to Bellamy up against that wall.

"Bellamy, I still need you for a few more minutes to get your solo shots," Parker shouts over his shoulder as we make our way back to his studio. I beeline for the dressing room, purposefully not glancing at Bellamy. I can't risk it. Who knows what I'm liable to do if tempted again.

On my own in the dressing room, I take my time wiping the oil off my skin and changing back into my own clothes. The marketing assistant from Monte's Manties pops in to say thanks and that I can keep the thong I wore. Not that it matters—I'll never be able to wear it again without remembering this shoot.

I take out my phone, check my flight status for tomorrow, check my email, check my DMs, anything to stall so I don't have to leave yet. I hear Bellamy coming before I see him and I start rooting around in my handbag like I'm busy getting my shit together, rather than loitering and waiting for him.

"You're still here," he says with a smirk. "Waiting for me?"

I pick up my handbag from the counter and plant my other hand on my hip. "Why the fuck would I do that?"

Bellamy's gaze flicks from my face to my bag and back again. Then he laughs like I amuse the hell out of him.

Fucker. Why am I doing this? Why can't I stop myself? "Where are you staying tonight?"

Bellamy's eyebrows shoot up. "Staying? I'm not staying in LA. I'm flying back to San Francisco."

Shit. That is not what I was expecting him to say. It throws a wrench in my plans for the evening. "Change your flight."

"What?" Bellamy chuckles, incredulously.

It's a ridiculous thing to ask, especially considering I wasn't really asking. I reach into the side pocket of my handbag and pull out my hotel room key card. It's still in the little paper sleeve with my room number written on it. I place it on the counter, the edge of the card snapping against the hard surface, and with one finger, I push it in Bellamy's direction.

"Change your flight," I say with more meaning in my voice this time. "I fly out of LAX at ten tomorrow morning. We can share a cab."

Bellamy's jaw drops and delight bubbles up in me at the sight. I've surprised him. Shocked him. Stunned him into silence. Who knew Bellamy-The Golden Boy-Blais who always has the perfect retort to everything, could actually be speechless.

His gaze shoots from the card to me. "You're not serious."

I shrug. I'm deadly serious and if Bellamy can't figure that out, then... well, fuck, I really hope he figures it out. But that's up to him. I've put the invitation out there, it's his decision what to do with it.

———

I've been flipping through boring TV channel after boring TV channel for hours and there's still no sign of Bellamy. Am I waiting for something that's not going to happen? Perhaps I should've been clearer. *Come to my hotel room, Bellamy. I want to fuck.*

It shouldn't take him this long to change and grab his own cab to the hotel. He should've been thirty minutes behind me, max.

Fuck this. I'm not waiting around for some asshole to maybe show up if he maybe feels like it. If I can't have Bellamy's ass tonight, then I'll go out and find another one. Checking that I have my wallet, my phone, and the second key card for my room, I stride toward the door. I wrench it open and freeze.

Bellamy's standing on the other side, key card in hand like he was moving to tap it against the sensor. His chin is lowered and he peers up at me through his lashes. A stray curl lays haphazardly over his forehead.

Dipshit. Making me wait this long. I grab the front of his shirt and haul him inside. He's laughing when my lips land on his. He's still laughing as I stumble backward, his hands coming around my waist to keep us upright. I land against a wall and the impact knocks the air out of my lungs.

"Jesus, take it easy," Bellamy murmurs against my mouth.

Fucker. He wasn't the one idling away in a random hotel room wondering whether he'd made a huge fucking mistake. I shove him away from me. Bellamy and his smug-ass grins. He backs off, hands raised in surrender.

"Did you change your flight?" I ask. Because there's no point in him coming here if he didn't.

"Flight changed, as ordered."

Ha. As if the asshole has ever done anything he's been told. I stalk over to the minibar and the bottle of whiskey I had room service send up earlier. It's not as good as the stuff I have at home, but it'll do in a pinch. I hand one glass to Bellamy as I pass him on my way to the window.

"Thanks…"

His reflection in the window is clear enough for me to see the confusion on his face. I don't try to clarify anything for him. I couldn't even if I wanted to. I'm equally confused by my irrational behavior. Not only irrational—emotional. It's like every ounce of common sense I possess evaporates into thin air whenever Bellamy gets involved. A mention of his name, a flash of his picture, a tickle of a memory—any little thing remotely related to him turns me into this raging mass of feelings and hormones that I have no control over.

He sips the whiskey as his gaze travels around the room. It's not really a room, actually. It's a suite. Even then, there's only so much to look at before he returns to me. I'm still by the window, back to him, watching his reflection, because I'm not sure I trust myself to do anything else.

"Are you okay?"

No. I'm really not. Not when it comes to Bellamy Blais.

# CHAPTER
# FOURTEEN

## BELLAMY

I'm trying to remember why I thought it was a good idea to come to Noel's hotel room—suite. There must've been a good reason. Otherwise, why would I eat the last-minute flight change fee? It's not like I have extra cash to throw around like Noel does.

But standing here, being very thoroughly ignored, I'm seriously doubting my good sense.

Noel's shoulders tighten at my question. He doesn't seem okay, but it's hard to tell. He's always so ornery that this might be within a standard deviation of his average.

I take another sip of the very good whiskey Noel always manages to have on hand and help myself to a seat on the plush, upholstered sofa. It's embroidered and gilded and the wooden claw feet are polished to a shine. The curtains on the windows are heavy and tapestry-like, held back with tasseled rope. The TV is one of those things that masquerade as a famous painting when not in use. And on the far side of the room is a set of French doors that open onto the darkened bedroom. Not Noel's typical style, I think, but the whole place still reeks of wealth.

"Did you invite me over here just to ignore me all night? Because the least you could do is feed me. And I'm definitely going to sleep on the couch or something. I'm not about to pay for another hotel room now."

Noel sighs and his posture goes slack. I've never seen it do that before, I realize. He's always so high-strung, so tightly wound. I didn't think he was capable of relaxing. He picks up a leather-bound binder from the round dining table in a corner and brings it to me.

"Order whatever you want."

My eyes nearly fall out of my head at the prices on the room service menu. The breakfast options cover three whole pages, from a bowl of fruit to steak and eggs. The cheapest burger is forty bucks. There's even caviar sold by the ounce. Jesus. I could squeeze out two weeks of groceries with the cost of one meal from this menu—without having to resort to ramen. It'd be cheaper to get Uber Eats or Door Dash.

I can't order from room service, not at these prices. "How about going out somewhere? There's an In-and-Out not too far away."

The look Noel gives me is so filled with revulsion I have to laugh. My guess is he's never been to an In-and-Out. He's probably never been to any fast-food joint in his life. How can food be edible if it's not prepared by a Michelin-starred chef?

He holds out his hand for the binder, so I give it back to him.

"What do you want?" he asks as he sets the binder down next to the suite's phone.

From that menu? Nothing. But Noel doesn't give me a chance to object again. His call has connected.

"Room service. We'll have the seared lamb with steamed vegetables and the sirloin with truffle fries."

There aren't even any normal fries—nope, there are only *truffle* fries.

Noel hangs up abruptly and it takes me a moment to realize the order's been placed. He didn't say please or thank you. Just barked what he wanted into the phone and dropped it back into its cradle.

I run a hand over my face. The person taking the order doesn't even know I'm here and I'm still cringing with embarrassment.

"What?" Noel asks when he spots me trying to hide behind my hand.

I shake my head. "Nothing." I'm not masochistic enough to try and explain manners to Noel.

He scowls, then paces back to the window—and back to ignoring me too, it seems. His gaze is trained on something out in the distance like he's doing everything he can to pretend I'm not here.

I go over and stand behind him, close enough to feel his body heat, which means he can feel mine too. He doesn't move away. His gaze doesn't waver. But his breath hitches and his shoulders tense. My nose almost brushes the shell of his ear and when I exhale, he shivers. His jaw is ticking, the muscle pulsing right beneath his ear.

I know why Noel invited me here tonight. It's the same reason I took him up on the invitation. There's something between us, something confusing and strange that neither of us understand, but neither of us can ignore. It's what drives us to message each other endlessly when we could easily stop. It's that zinging feeling that runs through me when I see him, when I'm in the same room as him. Whatever this is—chemistry, attraction, foolishness—we're both helpless in the face of it.

I press my lips to the corner of Noel's jaw where it's clenched tight. His eyes flutter shut and he exhales, expelling all the tension he holds in his body.

*That's it. Give in to it. Give in to us.*

My lips move behind his ear, then down his neck. Noel tilts his head the other way to give me more room. I sink my teeth gently into the tendons running down to his shoulder. He melts back against me and I circle my arms around his waist, drawing him closer.

This is a different Noel. One I haven't seen before or even knew existed. Soft and malleable and liquid. Save for his cock, which is hard and raging behind the zipper of his tight black pants. I grope him and he presses himself into my palm. My hips inch forward until my own erection is nestled in his ass. He reaches back, one hand on my hip to urge me on, the other to the back of my head as he turns to kiss me over his shoulder. The kiss is gentle too, made up of tiny licks with the tips of our tongues. I sigh into it and Noel drinks down the sound.

I think I like this version of Noel. I suspect this might be the real thing underneath all the sharp edges and abrasive walls he throws up.

I turn him around, or maybe he turns himself around, and his arms go to my shoulders. His fingers go into my hair, curling around the strands, nails on my scalp. I slip my hands up the back of his shirt and flatten one palm along the dip of his lower back. With the other, I trace up the valley of his spine. His skin is smooth like silk and goosebumps break out across my forearms at the sensation.

Our tongues dance. Slow and unhurried, savoring and tasting, until I'm breathless and a little unsteady on my feet. Noel's breathless too, chest rising and falling rapidly as we lean our foreheads together. I can almost hear the thoughts racing through his head.

*Bellamy's my rival. I don't like him. Why am I doing this?*

Tension trickles back into his body. His muscles stiffen under my palms and his weight shifts to lean away from me. I tighten my arms around him and capture his mouth again. I've finally gotten Noel all relaxed and pliable, I'm not about to lose him to his overthinking.

A knock on the door makes Noel jump and he pushes me away like we've been caught by our parents or the paparazzi.

"It's just room service, remember?" I say, my voice a little hoarse from our kisses.

He clamps his jaw shut again and nods jerkily. His hands are in fists by his side. I go to answer the door.

A young guy dressed in a hotel uniform rolls a cart into the room. It's laden with round silver domes that he arranges on the table, complete with full place settings. He pours two glasses of ice water, then two glasses of red wine from a decanter.

"This is a 2011 La Dame de Montrose Bordeaux from Chateau Montrose. Complimentary. From the chef." He sets the decanter off to the side. "Anything else I can get for you?"

"No. That's all." Noel's voice is tight, but he walks over with a folded bill in his hand. I think I see a fifty on the corner.

The porter takes it with a nod and a knowing smile before bowing out.

When the door snicks shut behind him, I turn back to Noel. "Hungr—"

I don't get to finish the word. Noel's on me like he's starving and I'm the gourmet meal the porter just served up. His tongue is in my mouth, his hands tug on the hem of my shirt, and he's dragging me toward the darkened bedroom.

Gone is the sweet tenderness of a moment ago. This Noel is the force of nature I'm used to. He pulls my shirt off my head, then reaches for my jeans, unbuttoning them and sliding down the fly as deftly as if they were on his legs instead of mine. He reaches in. And stops.

The dark pools of his eyes narrow into accusatory slits. "Commando?"

I smile and tilt my hips to press my erection into his hand. "My underwear got lost somewhere on set."

Noel squeezes me. Hard. A shudder runs through me and my groin tightens with desire. I wrap my fingers around the back of Noel's neck and crash our mouths together again. He catches my bottom lip between his teeth and bites. The pain rushes down to my cock, making it pulse against Noel's palm. He lets out a satisfied groan as he squeezes me again.

He drops to his knees suddenly, taking my jeans with them, and all at once my cock is in his mouth. His teeth are hooked right behind the ridge of the glans, and the threat of those sharp edges, of that powerful jaw, makes me leak pre-cum all over his tongue. Noel sucks it all down then digs his tongue into my slit for more.

"Jesus Christ," I breathe.

I don't even know if this qualifies as a blowjob. It feels like my cock has been caught in some kind of twisted vacuum hose turned up on high. Noel sucks my dick right to the back of his mouth, right down his throat with no sign of a gag reflex. Before I can even process the incredibly tight pressure, he's back at the tip again, tongue burrowing like he's trying to sound me. Goddamn, it's intense and fast, an onslaught of pleasure up and down my length that has my knees going weak.

My orgasm marches toward me, steady and unrelenting. "Fuck, Noel. Goddamn." I push at his shoulders and pull on his hair, stumbling backward when he releases me and collapsing on the bed.

Noel rises to his feet. His face is a wreck with makeup smudged around his eyes and running down his cheeks. His hair stands up on end. Half his face is wet with spittle and his shirt is covered in splotches of dark fabric.

My insides twist at the sight of him. My heart pounds against my ribs. Hot isn't enough to describe Noel. Sexy doesn't cut it. Bad boy, dangerous, and edgy come a little closer, but they're not quite right either. There's something magnetic about him, it's ephemeral and elusive, hard to pin down or describe. But anyone who's ever seen him like this knows what I'm talking about. He snags them, draws them in, and never lets them go.

That's what he's done to me, without me realizing it. All this time, he's been raging at me, attacking me, trying to tear me down, and still he's managed to ensnare me. I'm caught. I've fallen. I'm obsessed.

He unbuttons his tight leather pants, shimmying out of them before tossing them aside. Next goes his shirt, which slides off his shoulders and lands on the floor. I scooch back on the bed as Noel climbs up. His eyes are sharp and focused, trained laser-like on my face. He plants his knees on either side of my legs as he moves over me, like a predator going after his prey.

When his face is level with mine, we stare into each other's eyes and electricity arcs between us. It zings through me, lighting me up until every inch of my body feels alive and on fire. That's what Noel does. He electrifies and shocks me into a different plane of reality that I didn't know was possible before I met him. And now that I know what it's like to have him, to taste him, to feel his body against mine, I don't think I can ever go back.

## CHAPTER
# FIFTEEN

## NOEL

Bellamy moves fast, rising up and tipping me over until our positions are reversed. I'm on my back, legs spread, his hips wedged between my thighs. His weeping cock glides alongside mine, sending shivers of bone-deep pleasure through me.

I don't think I'll ever get used to how my body responds to his every touch, his every word. Bellamy's got me all figured out. He knows where my buttons are and he's not afraid to press one after another after another.

His mouth is on mine but he's not kissing me the way I want him to. I want to suck on his tongue. I want him to suck on mine. But he teases me with flirty little licks before pulling away, leaving me no choice but to go after him.

That's what I've been doing for the past five years, running after Bellamy, trying to chase him down. Every time I think I've caught him, he always manages to wriggle out of my hands and stay one step ahead of me.

Not this time though. This time, I've got him in my

grasp and I'm not letting go. I grab the back of his head and crush our lips together. I shove my tongue between his teeth until he sucks on it like I want him to. When he moans, I plant one foot on the mattress and roll us again.

I lay every ounce of my weight on him. I scrape my teeth along his jaw, down his throat. He digs his nails into my ass and when he squeezes, our cocks rub against each other. God, that shouldn't feel so damn good.

"Fuck, Noel."

He pulls my ass cheeks wide, exposing my hole to the cool air in the room. I clench, my hole suddenly hungry for cock, desperate to be filled. The need roars inside me, so loud and intense that it stuns me into inaction. I press my face against Bellamy's neck as I writhe, searching for something to satisfy this unrestrained craving.

He takes my momentary distraction to flip us yet again and this time, he doesn't hesitate to wrap his lips around my nipple. The one with the bar piercing. He flicks it with his tongue, pushing it left and right under my skin, and when he tugs it with his teeth, tingles spread from my chest across my entire body. I arch up, cock pulsing and leaking, hot and heavy on my stomach. When Bellamy's teeth sink into my flesh, a gush of pre-cum spills out of my dick.

"Ahh," I cry out. My voice is gravelly from the blowjob I gave him and thick with feelings I don't want to acknowledge. Like I need him. I want him. More than I'll ever admit out loud, more than I even want to admit silently to myself. It's the truth though, no matter how vehemently I try to deny it. Bellamy's a drug and I'm hooked.

"Please."

He gazes up at me through those dark blond lashes and smiles his smug little smile. He knows exactly what he's doing to me. He knows exactly how to take me apart. I hate it.

I hate it and need it at the same time.

"Please what?"

I glower at him. He fucking knows what. He has all along. He only wants me to say it out loud so we both know he's won. That he always fucking wins.

"Fuck me," I bite out through clenched teeth.

He cocks an eyebrow and his smile widens into a grin that he ghosts over my ear as he whispers to me. "Fuck you, huh? That's why you asked me to come tonight, isn't it? You want this thick cock in your tight little asshole?" He shifts and the tip of his dick slips under my balls, running right over my guiche and my hole.

I shiver and whimper and spread my legs wider for him. It's wanton and I'm not usually this shameless for anyone. Bellamy's the exception. He's always been the exception.

He turns me onto my stomach and I bury my face into a pillow, relief and anticipation ratcheting up inside me. His lips land on the back of my neck, soft and tender, like a warm towel melting away all my aches. His fingers trail feather light down my back, sending goosebumps racing across my skin. My stomach tightens when he nudges my legs apart to kneel between them, and my hole twitches when he blows a stream of air across it.

He plants a kiss on my tailbone, then an inch lower and an inch lower still, until he can seal his lips around my hole and swirl his tongue over it. My back arches, begging for more, but he doesn't give it to me. Instead, he travels lower to my taint, drawing patterns and flicking my piercing with his tongue.

"Mmm," he hums.

I buck as pleasure rushes through me, overwhelming, making my vision flash white behind my eyelids. "Bellamy," I sob. I'm gripping fistfuls of sheets. I can't keep my hips on the bed. My toes curl so hard the muscles in my feet might spasm.

Bellamy nuzzles the back of my balls with his nose and takes a noisy, deep inhale. He's smelling me. Jesus Christ. Raw, primal lust slams into me and my balls pulse, swollen and heavy and so fucking sensitive.

"Bellamy, please." I can't take anymore. I'm going to explode if he doesn't get inside me. I'm going to come apart. I'm going to die.

He's chuckling when he covers my back with his body. But when he whispers into my ear this time, his voice is as tortured as my own. "Lube. Condoms."

It takes me a solid few seconds to figure out what he's talking about, then I wave my hand in the direction of the bathroom. "Toiletry bag."

Bellamy flies off the bed and returns before I have a chance to miss him, my entire toiletry bag in his hand. He rummages through it, pulls out what we need, and drops the rest on the floor. His fingers are already slick with lube by the time he climbs between my legs again.

"Hurry," I say. I bring my knees up under me to present my ass to him. But he doesn't hurry. He takes his time circling my hole and easing his fingers into my body. He's gentle as he opens me up and stretches me. I don't need him to be gentle though. I don't need this careful preparation. I want it hard and fast. I want it to hurt.

"Hurry!"

I think the asshole slows down even more. He twists his fingers and taps lightly on my prostate. He adds a third finger and does it all again. By the time he finally tears open the goddamn condom wrapper, my knees are shaking and I'm one thrust away from coming.

That thrust never comes. Instead, Bellamy is just as careful and tender as he feeds his cock into me. I feel every inch of him sliding past that ring of muscle. I feel myself adjust and give way to his invasion. It's all so slow that my senses have time to process every sensation, to dwell on each signal sent back to my brain. It drives me to the edge and beyond, it overloads all my senses until I can't think, can't breathe, can't function. I can only exist.

Bellamy doesn't stop when he bottoms out. He keeps pressing forward until I'm flat on my stomach. His body covers me entirely, his legs tangle with mine, and his fingers close around my hands. His weight pins me to the mattress. And then he stays like that, unmoving, spearing me open and holding me still. "Fuck, Noel."

I want to be angry at him. I want to shout and rage and fight so he has no choice but to fuck me into submission. But that fury has abandoned me, leaving me with tears seeping out of my eyes. This is too much. I can't. This isn't what I want. This isn't what I was asking for when I invited him over.

The pillow under my face is drenched when Bellamy finally moves. Tiny little rolls of his hips that wreck me with their intimacy. This isn't fucking. This is barely sex. This goes deeper, demands more, penetrates to the core of a person. It's unvarnished and bare. It's potent and powerful.

It soaks into every crack and crevice until I'm fully saturated, until there's no room for anything else. No bitterness, no hate. I have no choice but to surrender to this thing between us, to succumb to its demands.

I drag my hand down to my chest, bringing Bellamy's arm with me so he's holding me tighter. Then I slide one knee up and to the side so he can fill me even more. He exhales a shaky breath by my ear and squeezes my hands.

"Noel." He feels it too. It's not only me. He's just as overcome as I am.

We move together now, our bodies falling into a rhythm like this is something we've done since eternity. His cock slides in and out of my hole, sending surges of electricity rippling through me. I clench down on him, making him moan and curse behind me. I'm already over-stimulated, my nerve endings too overloaded to spark an orgasm. And yet the pressure builds in my groin, in my balls, running up the length of my cock.

Sweat drips off us. It makes a wet, squelching sound as our bodies move against each other. Bellamy's cheek is pressed, sticky and hot, against mine and our breaths mingle with every gasping inhale and shaky exhale.

The climax that eventually overtakes me is a blessed release. It shoots me up into the stratosphere where the air is thin and gravity is weak. It bursts through every cell in my body like the vacuum of space is tearing me apart. I don't exist anymore, not in a way I understand. I'm not bones and flesh and organs. I'm ecstasy, bliss, and joy.

I black out at some point, lost to the serenity of things that I don't have words to describe. I float in and out of consciousness, each time reaching for Bellamy's warm body before slipping away again.

The next time I reach for him, I only find cold sheets and I lurch awake. The room is pitch black. The digital clock on the nightstand blinks two-something in the morning. I'm under the covers, but alone in the big bed.

A sound comes from the suite's living room. Bellamy.

I find him sitting at the table with our abandoned dinner. He's stark naked, scrolling through his phone while munching on the cold, limp fries.

He glances up and when he sees me, I tug the two sides of the hotel bathrobe tighter around me. His lips twitch and I know what he's thinking. He's seen it all already. He's touched it all already. There's no point in trying to cover any of it up. But he doesn't say any of that. He just pushes the plate of fries in my direction.

I pull out the other chair at the table and sit. No aches, no soreness. Either we were incredibly docile with our fucking earlier or my body is still high on endorphins. Maybe both.

"You're not hungry?" Bellamy asks, taking another fry and popping it into his mouth.

My stomach growls. "The fries are cold," I protest. "Room service is twenty-four hours. We can get a fresh plate."

Bellamy's brow furrows. "No, we don't. These are perfectly good." He nudges the plate toward me again. "Try one."

I can never back down when he issues me a challenge. I take a fry and nibble on it. It's cold and mushy and… oddly satisfying.

"See?" Bellamy smiles, as smug and egotistical as ever.

Except the annoyance I feel is minimal, tempered with something giddy followed by a blossoming warmth. "I'd still rather have fresh ones," I say with an exaggerated frown.

He laughs and the familiar sound threads through me the way it's always done in the past. But my hackles don't rise, I don't itch with irritation. Something that feels like a smile tugs at my lips before I manage to shut it down.

"You haven't lived if you haven't eaten day-old fries." He's teasing me. Like he always has.

I reach for the frustration, the infuriation, but it's gone. And it kind of feels nice.

Not that I'm ever going to tell Bellamy that. I drag the plate closer to me and take another fry.

# CHAPTER
# SIXTEEN

## BELLAMY

Santino is in the kitchen, looking skeptically into the refrigerator, when I get home. "Hey, there's nothing to eat. Wanna order a pizza?" he asks, shutting the fridge door.

"Uh, sure. I'm good with whatever."

"Cool. Prepare for anchovies."

I chuckle under my breath but leave him to order. Santino really does like anchovies, but he knows better than to put them on my half of the pizza.

My phone rings before I can do anything but set my stuff down. Mom's face fills the screen.

"Hey, Mom."

"Hello, dear. How are you?"

I flop down on my bed and stare at the ceiling. That's a simple question that only needs a simple answer, and yet I don't know what to tell her. I'm reeling from the trip to Los Angeles, the intensity of the photo shoot, and then the even more intense night in Noel's hotel room. It was only supposed to be a booty call, another tick on the bedpost tallies we're both keeping. But it turned into something a whole lot more.

I've never had sex with anyone like that before. Where I couldn't tell where I ended and he began. Where my orgasm wasn't merely a physical thing, but a religious experience. And afterward, sitting at that table in the wee hours of the morning, sharing a plate of cold fries. Something changed between us. Something fundamental to who we are to one another.

We went back to bed after eating, curled up in each other's arms, and fell asleep. When the sun finally came up, we moved around the bathroom like we'd been doing it together for years. My hand on his waist as I squeezed past him. His hand brushing mine when he passed me the toothpaste. Noel called for a car to take us to the airport and I bought us breakfast at one of the restaurants in the terminal.

Right before he boarded, I grabbed his phone and sent myself a text. So now we have each other's phone numbers. No more DMs over social media.

"Dear?"

I fling my arm over my eyes. "Fine. Good. You?"

"I'm doing okay," she says, followed immediately by a bout of coughing. Mom sighs.

I sigh too. "And Dad?"

"He's…"

Yeah, I get it. He's never doing well. The doctors never have a silver bullet. We're forever stuck in this limbo of chronic illness.

Mom clears her throat to break the silence. "Anyway, Twyla met with a college scout this week."

The news makes me perk up with a mix of elation and anxiety. "For volleyball? Which school?"

"Grantham University. Have you heard of it before?"

My knowledge of post-secondary education is a half-step above nothing. I know Stanford and Berkley are rivals and that even the cheapest school was out of my price range back then. But not out of Twyla's—I won't let that happen.

"No, I haven't. Where is it?"

"Upstate New York. Near Rochester."

I only have a vague sense of where Rochester is. North, I think. "So it's a small school?"

"Yes, it's one of those… fancy schools."

Meaning expensive. Small and elite and requiring a fortune to attend. "Did she speak with anyone else?"

"I think so, but this is the only one she's told me about."

Which means this is the one Twyla wants to go to. Great.

"It's a good school," Mom continues like she's trying to argue Twyla's case for her. Except the more she talks, the lower my heart sinks. "It ranks well against its peers. Its graduates have high employment rates. Some of them are quite prestigious."

"That's awesome," I say. I really am excited for my baby sister. It's fantastic that she's getting interest from this kind of school and I want her to have all the opportunities I never had.

But I also have a very realistic grasp of the balance of my bank account and how far it can stretch. It might be sitting pretty right now, but it won't stay that way with tuition bills coming in every few months. So I take a deep breath and ask the question I know both Mom and I are dreading.

"How much is tuition?"

"Well…" Her hesitation doesn't bode well. "The scholarship should cover most of the tuition…"

Yeah, that's what I thought. Even with the scholarship, it'll be a lot. Plus living expenses since she'll have to move halfway across the country. My stomach sinks. My whole body feels weighed down, like I'm being pulled under the surface after only just learning how to tread water.

It's been like this ever since Dad got sick. I hustle and work my ass off to make enough so we're comfortable. Then the unexpected happens or something comes up and suddenly I'm scrambling again. It's never enough. I can never stay ahead. I'm always playing catch-up.

One part of my mind starts listing off ways I can pad my finances—more studio gigs, more product sponsorships. I've already upped the subscription price on my OnlyFans page and I'm offering Cameos at a premium.

Another part of my mind wants to throw up its hands and surrender. It wants to wallow in self-pity and sob about how unfair life is.

"Dear?"

"Yeah, I'm here."

"I don't want you to worry."

I huff silently. Telling me not to worry is about as effective as telling Dad not to cough.

"Twyla's working all summer at the grocery store and she's staying on part-time during the school year. I've been filling in every now and then when a teacher calls in sick. We're not entirely dependent on you."

Perhaps not. But then, we both know that Twyla's

minimum wage job as a cashier and Mom picking up substitute teaching shifts a few times a month isn't going to cut it, not in any significant way. I'll have to pick up the slack. Like I always do.

We eventually hang up and the first thing I do is tap on the little red bubble telling me I have unread text messages—they're from Noel. My heart skips a beat, then races away as bubbles of giddy excitement fill my chest.

NOEL

You forgot something.

Followed by a picture of the jockstrap I wore during the photo shoot. I stuffed it in his suitcase before we left the hotel. It's a silly thing. A ridiculous thing. But for some unknown reason, my eyes start filling with tears.

Los Angeles feels so far away and so long ago. Those hours with Noel are like a dream, fantastical and unreal, when everything is simple and straightforward. I'm attracted to him and he's attracted to me. We're explosive together and all that matters is chasing the high of the next orgasm.

There are no family obligations when I'm with Noel. There are no financial burdens to consider. Noel is an indulgence, a guilty pleasure, a secret escape where I can hit pause on life.

BELLAMY

Thought you'd like a souvenir.

NOEL

Not memorable enough to need one.

Liar.

*middle finger emoji* *smirk-face emoji*

I don't know why I do what I do next. The action never crosses my conscious mind. I don't decide to tap on Noel's name and then tap on the call button. It just happens.

The call only rings once before Noel picks up and a tear escapes the corner of my eye. The image of his face on my screen dislodges the weight on my shoulders, and I drag in a shaky breath like he's brought me to the surface of the water.

He's smirking, like he knew I would call him. His dark eyes dance mischievously with an unspoken, "I told you so." A pang of longing hits my chest so hard I gasp. I miss him. I wish he was here. Or I'm there. Or we're back in LA. I wish I could lose myself in him for a little longer, put off life for another day. The longing is so potent, so tangible that another tear escapes.

Noel's smirk turns into a scowl. "What's wrong?"

I shake my head and swipe at the wetness on my cheeks. "Nothing."

"Fuck that. Why are you crying if nothing's wrong?"

The fact that he curses at me while trying to figure out why I'm crying is so quintessentially Noel that I laugh out loud. Which only makes him scowl harder and makes me miss him more.

"Jerk face, answer me when I ask you a question."

I don't know where to start. And it's not like Noel would understand anyway. He doesn't have a sick dad or a worried mom or a kid sister he wants to send to college. His life is so completely opposite to mine it's laughable.

"Why do you cam?" I ask him instead. He clearly doesn't need the money. If it's about fame and prestige,

I'm sure he could get that without taking his clothes off for a camera. Being a camboy isn't usually at the top of every kid's *What I Want to Be When I Grow Up* list.

Noel's eyes narrow suspiciously. "Why do you want to know?"

I lift a shoulder then drop it. "Because I want to know. Can't I be curious?"

He glares through the phone at me like I'm going to sell his secrets to the highest-bidding tabloid.

"Fine, don't tell me. Whatever."

He harrumphs. "There's nothing to tell. I do it because my parents hate it."

His answer makes my eyebrows shoot up to my hairline. "You what?"

Noel gives a half-hearted shrug. "My parents couldn't care less about what I do with my life. The only thing they care about is their public image and having a camboy for a son is embarrassing."

I stare at his face in disbelief. "So you do porn to embarrass your parents?"

"Yeah," he says like it's the most logical thing in the world. "Why do *you* do porn?"

I open my mouth and shut it again because my answer feels so pedestrian in comparison. "Well, it also has to do with my parents."

"Are you trying to embarrass them too?"

"Uh, no, I'm not. The opposite, in fact."

Noel cocks an eyebrow. "You're trying to make them proud by being the best camboy the world's ever seen?"

The sarcasm and flippancy of his not-funny joke are exactly what I need right now. Some banter and verbal sparring to make everything feel not quite so dire and impossible.

"Fuck you, you rich, entitled bastard."

Noel practically preens at the insult. "Don't say it if you don't mean it."

"Asshole."

"I never claimed to be anything else."

I can't keep the smile off my face. And it's not the practiced camera-ready smile either. It's one that comes from someplace deep inside, so filled with genuine happiness that tears prickle my eyes again.

Jesus. Fuck. I blink a couple times to fight them back.

"Bellamy, seriously. What's wrong?" Noel's voice is low now, with not a trace of teasing or biting edge.

I hesitate, still not sure whether this is the direction I want our sort-of, not-really relationship to go. "You seriously want to know?"

He gives me a look fierce enough to travel across space and time and pin me to the spot. "Don't make me fly all the way out there to make you tell me."

He wouldn't. Would he? There's something in his eyes that makes me think that yes, he absolutely would.

I take a deep breath and let go of the worries I clutch so tightly to me all the time. Then I tell him everything he wants to know.

# CHAPTER
# SEVENTEEN

## NOEL

The guys are talking around me while I absentmindedly spin my mimosa glass in a circle on the table. Actually, no, I'm not absentminded—I'm preoccupied. With Bellamy.

He's been at the forefront of my every thought since we left the hotel in Los Angeles. The weight of his body covering mine, the fullness of having him deep inside me, the sticky press of our cheeks. I thought I was fixated on him before, but that is nothing compared to this all-consuming obsession.

And then our phone call. The brightness went out of his eyes as he talked about his family's finances. His shoulders drooped like the weight he carried was too heavy. Seeing him like that made my hackles rise in protectiveness and my mind immediately launched into all the ways I could fix things for him.

Did his dad need an at-home nursing service? I could pay for that. Did he want to start a college fund for Twyla? I could seed one for him. I was *this close* to offering him a card on my credit card account. The only thing that held me back was the flash of pride in Bellamy's eyes as he explained how he single-handedly kept his family afloat all these years.

But that doesn't mean I'm going to sit back and do nothing. I just need to find the right thing—something that Bellamy won't balk at accepting.

"How was the photo shoot?"

I realize a beat too slowly that the question was directed toward me. Three pairs of eyes stare at me, waiting for an answer.

"It was fine." My voice is pretty steady, but something about how I sound or how I look tips Sebastian off.

He cocks his head and narrows his eyes. "Just fine?"

"Yeah, fine." Except my voice is tighter this time and I shift in my seat before I can stop myself.

Sebastian straightens and zeros in on me with a stern look. I'm not getting out of this interrogation unscathed.

"What happened?"

Rhys and Hayden look between me and Sebastian, but they're not coming to my rescue.

"Nothing." I try to deny it one more time, setting my face into my best "leave me alone" pout.

But Sebastian knows me too well to be intimidated. He doesn't even bother asking again, merely folds his hands on the table and waits. The silence drags on, growing heavier by the second. I'm usually pretty good at these kinds of staring contests, and Sebastian tends to cave before I do, but all the circling thoughts about Bellamy have thrown me off my game today.

"Fine, Jesus, something happened." A shit ton of stuff happened, way more than I'm willing to share at the moment. I barely understand it myself and if I tell the guys, they'll never stop with the questions.

"There was someone else at the photo shoot."

Rhys leans forward, curiosity lighting up his eyes. "Ooo, who was it? It wasn't Bellamy Blais, was it? Oh my god, that would be too funny."

Goddamn it.

Rhys gasps and squeals when he sees my expression darken. "Oh my god, it was Bellamy Blais!"

"Seriously?" Sebastian's practically out of his seat in surprise.

"Holy shit!" Hayden's eyes are as wide as saucers.

"Wait, was it just, like, you crossed paths? Or was there something more?" Rhys clearly wants there to be more.

"They made us do the shoot together," I finally admit.

"Like, *together* together?" Hayden's eyes can't possibly get any bigger.

"Like, standing next to each other? In the same photo?" Sebastian looks aghast, like we were asked to torture baby animals.

"Yeah, something like that." My very unhelpful imagination brings up memories of us in that studio, wearing nothing but tiny scraps of cloth, staring each other down, grappling with each other. My dick stirs, remembering where that had led.

"Why would they do that?" Hayden asks, ever the innocent one.

Rhys casts him a sympathetic look. "Really? It's not obvious?"

"Actually, it's kind of brilliant." Sebastian's bouncing now, eyes darting around as his mind whirs, conjuring up a scheme I'm sure I'm going to regret. He glides his hand through the air like it's a theater marquee. "A legendary rivalry. The ultimate face-off. Mortal enemies battle it out —who will win?"

"That's a little much, don't you think?" I grouse because he's hitting much too close to the truth for my comfort.

"I'd watch that." Rhys nods.

"So would I," Hayden agrees.

I shoot them all hard glances. "There's nothing to watch. It's just photos."

"Oh, but what if there was?" Sebastian's already three steps ahead and I'm scrambling to catch up.

"What the hell is that supposed to mean?"

He's on his phone, tapping away at god knows what. "Do you think he'll do it?"

"Who? Do what?"

"Bellamy Blais. Do you think he'll do a video?"

Oh, Christ. I can't believe I didn't see this coming from a mile away. "You want to shoot a video with Bellamy?"

Rhys pounces. "It's just 'Bellamy' now, is it?"

I realize my mistake. I've never called him only by his first name. It's always Bellamy Blais, or more often, Bellamy fucking Blais. It's only since we started our... thing... that he's become more than an amorphous name and face I love to hate so much.

He's more than a sunny disposition and a golden smile. More than an egotistical, arrogant camboy who thinks he's better than everyone else. I thought he was bent on climbing the celebrity ladder—and he is, but for more than merely fame and fortune.

It sounds ridiculous when I think about it now, how much I thought I knew about the guy when I'd barely met him. But people are more complicated than that. I should've known.

"Shut up," I throw at Rhys. That's the harshest retort I can come up with on the spot because Bellamy seems to have turned me soft.

"You should definitely do a video with Bellamy Blais," Hayden chimes in.

"No," I say, but no one is listening to me.

"It would be huge," Sebastian says without lifting his gaze from his phone. "Bigger than me and Christian, for sure."

"Really?" Hayden sounds incredulous and I don't blame him.

Sebastian and his boyfriend—well, they weren't boyfriends back then—did a series of videos together that blew up the porn corner of the internet. It launched Sebastian into the next level of his career. It was what inspired The Camboy Network. Sebastian knows what he's talking about when it comes to business-y things.

"Yeah, think about it. Everyone's always pitting them against each other. Remember the convention in Las Vegas? The kink party? Even this photo shoot. Fans are gagging for more. So let's give it to them. Noel and Bellamy, not only talking shit or getting up in each other's faces, but going all the way." Sebastian's gaze is a little unfocused like he can already see the video in his mind.

"Going all the way? You mean hate fucking." Rhys is quick to clarify.

"You don't have to put it so crudely," Sebastian objects, but Rhys is right.

What he's proposing is a video of me and Bellamy hate fucking for the rest of the world to watch.

No. Absolutely not. My reaction is immediate, deep and visceral. Far stronger than what I felt when I learned about the photo shoot. Stronger even than showing up at the kink party to find Bellamy as their special guest.

Glaring at each other from across the room or posing for a photographer is one thing. Actually having sex with Bellamy on camera is something else entirely. Having him slide into my body, opening up for him, feeling him move inside me. The taste of him on my tongue, the scent of him in my nose. Being in his arms, hearing the sounds he makes.

No. No. No.

I don't want anyone to see the look on Bellamy's face when I swallow his cock. I don't want anyone to hear the way he babbles incoherently. I don't want anyone else to experience how raw, unvarnished, and primal we are when we're together. That's *mine*. Mine to savor, mine to enjoy. Every hitch in his breath, every tremor through his body, every time his eyes roll toward the back of his head in unadulterated pleasure—all of that is mine and I'm not sharing.

"No." The single syllable is hard and sharp and it brings the entire table to a standstill.

Sebastian's expression goes from surprised to confused to horror. "No, of course. If you're not comfortable with it, then it's definitely out of the question. I don't know what I was thinking. I just got caught up in the idea. I'm so sorry. Forget I mentioned it. Pretend I never brought it up."

My chest feels like there's a vise around it, and my stomach is tangled up in a massive knot. I grind my teeth together until my jaw aches and my temples throb. Every nerve in my body is on edge.

The guys exchange concerned looks before slowly moving on to something else. I don't hear any of it. My mind is on Bellamy and the way he smiles at me like he knows exactly what I'm thinking. The way he laughs when I'm being stubborn. The heat of his palms when he touches me. I can taste the ocean on his skin and smell sunshine in his hair.

The weariness in his voice on the phone. The helplessness when he talked about his dad. The hopefulness when he bragged about his sister. Even now, my heart stutters at the memory, at how close I was to asking for his Venmo.

As much as I don't want to, as much as it twists me up inside and sets sparks to my anger, I know what I have to do.

I suck in a deep breath, forcing my lungs to expand against the vise around my chest. I wiggle my jaw side-to-side to relieve the tension. This isn't about me or what I want. I can be possessive and protective and selfish all day long, but I know guilt will find its way in somehow. Because as much as I'm desperate to keep Bellamy to myself, I want to wipe that look of exhaustion off his face even more.

Hayden calls for the bill and I numbly pull out my credit card. I don't even look at my receipt before scribbling on it and handing it back to the waiter. The guys shoot consoling glances at me as we file out of the restaurant. Rhys and Hayden wave goodbye and head off, but I grab Sebastian's arm before he can leave.

"Hey, um..." The words get caught in my throat.

"Noel, I'm so sorry about what I said in there. It won't happen again. I promise."

"No, that's not... I mean, it's a good idea." I hear the

words and it sounds like my voice, but it doesn't feel like I'm saying them. I feel like I'm standing next to myself, watching us in a conversation I don't want to have.

"Really?" Sebastian scrunches up his nose. He doesn't believe me. I don't blame him.

"Yeah, really. Can, uh—" I swallow and steel myself. "Can we talk about it some more?"

Sebastian studies me for several long moments, as if I might be playing a joke on him or something.

"I'm serious," I add, more assertively this time.

Sebastian still looks concerned, but he nods. "Yeah, okay. Let's talk."

# CHAPTER
# EIGHTEEN

## BELLAMY

I'm sitting in my room, door closed and laptop open, waiting for the video call to come through. Noel said he would be calling any minute now—he and his friend Sebastian Silver who runs The Camboy Network. It must be about some sort of collab, otherwise why in the world would Sebastian randomly want to meet with me? And if it *is* to talk about a collab, I'm pretty sure I know what they've got in mind.

A window pops up on my screen and I click on the green Accept button. Noel's face materializes and my heart does a fluttery-almost-uncomfortable flip in my chest. It's been doing that every time I see his face or hear his voice. It kind of feels like I'm scrambling to grab a hold of Noel, to latch on and lose myself in him, to never let go. It's weird. It's probably some unhealthy coping mechanism, but I can't bring myself to do anything but sink deeper into him.

"Hey." Noel adjusts the camera on his end and a

familiar face comes into view next to him. "This is Sebastian. Sebastian, Bellamy."

"Hey, Bellamy!" Sebastian waves at the camera. I've seen him before, of course. He's a decently big deal in the industry—not only as a camboy or performer, but as a director-producer. The Camboy Network is quickly building a reputation as a place where independent content creators want to be.

"Hi, nice to meet you."

"Same! I've heard so much about you!" Sebastian's smile stiffens a little and he shoots Noel a quick look before giving a small, slightly-nervous chuckle. "I just mean, you know, around and stuff. Not—"

"Okay," Noel cuts in with a scowl. "We get it."

"Right. Sorry. Anyway." Sebastian lights up again. "We want to talk to you about a potential collab."

Called it. And in fact, I called it right down to the details. Me and Noel, enemies in bed, hate fucking. It's the Monte's Manties photo shoot in live action.

I watch Noel's expression as Sebastian gives me the pitch. His jaw ticks and his lips are pressed into a straight line. He looks like he's trying to fight a frown, but he's losing badly. By the time Sebastian is done, Noel's exuding so much tension I can feel it all the way on the other side of the country.

"What do you think, Noel?" I ask when Sebastian finishes.

"I'm here, aren't I?" he spits out so forcefully that it pushes me back from the screen. Sebastian's eyebrows shoot up.

"Jesus, tell me how you really feel about it," I shoot back at him.

"Oh, fuck you."

Sebastian's expression goes wary, and honestly, I'm surprised. This doesn't sound like our normal banter—not even the type of back-and-forth Noel and I had before we started fucking. Noel's anger feels a lot more serious, a lot more genuine. It's not the type of toddler's temper tantrum that I love making fun of so much. This is real, heartfelt anger.

Which doesn't make any sense. He's the one facilitating this freaking meeting. If he was so vehemently against doing the collab, why bother bringing me and Sebastian together in the first place?

"Uh…" Sebastian's gaze flicks from Noel to me and back again. "I thought you guys were… you know, good. Together."

I fold my arms over my chest, intent on waiting Noel out on this one. I thought we were good too, but apparently, I was mistaken.

Noel drops his face into his hands and mutters, "fuck." His shoulders rise and fall a few times before he lifts his head again. "Yeah," he says with a huff. "I'm fine with it."

"Are you sure? You don't sound fine." I make sure there's enough taunting in my voice to get on Noel's nerves.

He sneers at me. "Yeah, I'm fucking fine."

"Okay!" Sebastian sounds artificially cheery, obviously trying to defuse whatever Noel and I have gotten ourselves into. "So, you guys can still pull off the 'I hate you' vibe. Good to know! Bellamy, obviously you don't have to give us an answer right now. I'll send over all the details and you can take some time to think it over. How's that sound?"

I unfold my arms and breathe out the tightness coiled inside me. "Sounds great."

Two minutes after I hang up with Sebastian and Noel, a text comes in.

NOEL

Sorry.

BELLAMY

What the fuck was that about?

Nothing.

I fling myself onto the bed and throw my arm over my eyes. A part of me—the petty part—wants to tell Noel to go fuck himself because I don't have time to put up with his volatile moods. But that would not be the smart move to make.

If Sebastian's numbers are accurate, a collab like this has the potential to make Fetish Studios's paycheck look like pocket change. Mom wouldn't have to keep picking up random teaching shifts. Twyla can go to that fancy college. It wouldn't solve all our money problems forever, but it would get us back to somewhere comfortable.

My phone buzzes again.

NOEL

Seriously. This is a good idea. You should say yes.

BELLAMY

Maybe I will. Just to piss you off.

Fuck you. The whole thing was my idea.

Sort of.

*eyebrow emoji* Yeah, sure. I'll believe
that in just about never. You're not that
smart.

Fine, fuck face. It was Sebastian's idea.
But I'm the one who told him to run
with it.

That, I do believe. I also believe that there's a good
intention buried somewhere in all of Noel's grumpiness.
Buried deep. So deep he can't even find it himself. Fucker.

NOEL

So you'll do it?

That is the question, isn't it? And suddenly the gravity
of the situation hits me. Am I ready to have sex with Noel
on camera? To have it all recorded and reproduced for
public consumption? What we have is explosive and hot
as hell, but there's more to it than that. Underneath the
rivalry and the chemistry, there's something growing
between us. It's small, not quite fully formed, but it's why
we text all the time, why we call each other almost every
day, why we keep drawing closer to one another when we
have all the reasons to stay the hell away.

Do I really want to put that on display for the whole
world to see? I mean, yeah, technically we're acting, but
let's be honest, neither of us are very good actors. I don't
think I'll be able to hide it when Noel slams into me, or
when I'm bottomed out inside him. This thing is too
powerful to ignore—it sucks me in until I'm drowning in
it, until I'm delirious with it.

It dawns on me then. That must be why Noel is so
ornery about the whole thing. He knows we won't be able

to avoid putting ourselves on display and he doesn't want to do it. My heart swells at the realization—he's doing this for me. There's no other reason why he would push forward with something he doesn't like, that he doesn't need.

I close my eyes and put a hand on my chest. The swell turns into an ache that I don't want to examine too closely. Instead, I pick up my phone again.

BELLAMY

Are you sure about this?

I can practically see Noel scowling as he reads the message. And I hear his reply in my ear, all growly and annoyed.

NOEL

Yes, I'm sure. Are you in or aren't you?

If Noel is willing to do this for me, if he's willing to be vulnerable and put himself out there, I'd be a fool to say no, right? The ache in my chest grows, bringing tears to my eyes. If Noel's willing to do this, then I have to be willing too.

BELLAMY

When and where?

———

The plane touches down on the tarmac and a light applause ripples through the cabin. "Ladies and gentlemen, welcome to Newark International Airport. The local time is…"

I still can't quite believe I'm here. Doing this. In the weeks since I agreed to the video, I've been trying to convince myself that Noel doesn't mean anything to me. We used to hate each other and now we don't. We might have fucked a few times, but we're nothing more than acquaintances with benefits. This is just another shoot, another collab with an industry professional. I've done this dozens of times before.

So why am I so nervous that my hands tremble? Why are my insides all twisted and cramped? Why is there this sense of dread and foreboding hanging over my head?

At the front of the plane, the flight attendant pushes open the door, and passengers all around me start grabbing their things. I pull out my phone and send a message to Noel.

BELLAMY

Landed. I'll be out soon.

NOEL

I'll meet you in the passenger pick-up zone. You can't miss me.

I feel like I'm walking to my own execution as I make my way through the terminal. And the worst part is not understanding why the fuck I feel this way. I can't put words to what exactly I'm afraid will happen, or why I've been equating this video to some kind of death sentence. All I know is I don't want to do this. It feels wrong, dangerous, bad.

Noel feels it too. I can tell from our calls that have grown more strained and stilted the closer we get to the filming date. Our banter has become flat and forced, painfully so. Sometimes we end up sitting on the phone, listening to each other breathe.

It's pathetically sappy, but those are the only times when it doesn't feel like I'm hurtling toward certain doom. The silence, knowing he's on the other end of the line, going through exactly what I'm going through—it's the one single solid thing I've been able to cling to. It's the lifeline and if I can just hold on tight enough, for long enough, maybe, just maybe, I'll come out the other side of this alive.

I walk faster. My demise might be waiting for me beyond those doors, but so is Noel. And once I'm with Noel, everything will be okay.

I'm practically jogging when I burst into the cool autumn air, dodging happy reunions and carts piled high with baggage. Noel said I wouldn't be able to miss him, but I don't see any sign of him. I'm about to send another text when a roar fills the air. I know before I look up.

A bright red Porsche convertible comes flying around the bend and squeals to a stop right in front of me. Noel's behind the wheel, hair mussed from the wind, sunglasses hiding his eyes, lips curled into a smolder that could melt a glacier. In that moment, no one else exists but the two of us, and I stumble toward the car as if he's physically pulling me closer.

Noel pushes the sunglasses to the top of his head and what I read in his eyes makes my heart stop. Longing. Need. A reckless abandonment of anything and everything except the undeniable attraction between us. He looks like he wants to devour me whole. I want to serve myself up to him. Maybe we can drive off in this outrageous sports car and disappear over the horizon.

"What is this, just a Porsche? Can't swing a Lamborghini?" The jab rolls off my tongue, easy and flowing, and the dark clouds above me start to thin.

Noel narrows his eyes and his lips twist into a smirk. "Parents took the Lambo this weekend."

I can't tell if he's joking, but if I had to guess, I'd say he wasn't. Of course his parents own a Lamborghini. I drop my duffle bag into the footwell of the decorative backseat, then slide into the passenger-side bucket seat that hugs me like a glove. The black leather upholstery is butter under my fingers and the engine purrs as it idles.

Noel reaches for my hand and twines our fingers together. He squeezes tight and I squeeze right back. Something unspoken passes through us, achingly sweet and bitter with relief. We're here. Together. Whatever comes next, we won't have to face it alone.

# CHAPTER
# NINETEEN

## NOEL

"Noel Carrington, we're going to be shooting a rivals hate fucking video today with Bellamy Blais. Are you excited?" Sebastian is behind the camera that's been set up in the living room for my intro interview.

We're in my family's house up in the Catskills, the one where the back of the house is made up of floor-to-ceiling windows overlooking green rolling hills and the river beyond. The trees have started turning color, their leaves a vibrant mix of reds and yellows and oranges.

The living room we're in is actually called the great room because of its double-height ceiling, enormous wrought iron chandeliers—that's right, plural—and the stone fireplace that's big enough for me to stand up in.

I give Sebastian my best "Are you fucking kidding me?" look in response to his question, and he chuckles.

"Right, of course."

At least that's one thing I don't have to lie about today. That initial gut reaction I had—the one where I wanted to set fire to the whole video collab idea—hasn't eased up at all in the weeks since Sebastian came up with it during brunch. If anything, it's gotten worse. It's a sour, churning feeling in my stomach. It's a heavy cloud of dread following me everywhere I go. When I'm on the phone with Bellamy, we sit there in silence like we're in mourning.

Seeing Bellamy in person helps, although the few hours we had to ourselves during the drive up to the house wasn't nearly enough. What I wouldn't give for a few days or weeks locked away with him somewhere where no one can find us.

I glance off to the left, past the camera, to where Bellamy's standing out of the way. He looks about as relaxed as I feel. Arms crossed, fingers digging into the muscle above his elbow. There's a tiny furrow in his brow that means he's worried, and I know exactly what he's thinking.

Neither of us want to do this, but we haven't talked about why. That's an area marked with a neon "danger zone" sign, and we want to go there even less than we want to shoot this video. So we're both gritting our teeth and sucking it up.

"What is it about Bellamy Blais that aggravates you so much?" Sebastian asks.

I twist my expression into a snarl. "His ego is too big for his dick."

Bellamy's lips twitch in amusement. Seeing it gives me a dose of soothing calm. Bickering is something we know how to do and we do it really fucking well. We just need to lean into what comes naturally and everything will be okay.

"The fucker thinks he's better than everyone."

"He's won a bunch of awards, so you could argue that he *is* better than everyone."

I huff out an unimpressed chuckle. "And how many people did he have to bend over for so they'd vote for him?"

Sebastian's jaw drops and his eyes go wide. Behind him, Sebastian's boyfriend—and for this weekend, our one-person crew—Christian, has his hand over his mouth to cover his laugh. Bellamy bursts out into a chortle and shakes his head with a smile that melts away some of my tightness. If nothing else, we'll be able to skewer each other with deadly precision all weekend. Sebastian can cut together a montage of insults.

"Too much?" I ask Sebastian.

"Uh…" He's stunned speechless. His innocent boy-next-door vibe could never handle the way Bellamy and I went at each other.

"It's fine," Bellamy calls out. "Keep going."

Sebastian takes a breath before continuing. "Okay, um, why did you agree to shoot this video?"

*Because Bellamy needs the money and he'll never accept a Venmo from me.*

"I want to wipe that swarmy grin off his face with my cock."

Sebastian looks scandalized, but Bellamy's smile grows wider. I force my hands open to ease the stiffness in my fingers and breathe out the pressure in my chest

"I'm sure we can work some face fucking into the video," Sebastian says with a wary tone.

"Good." I reach between my legs and grope myself. "I'm going to make him choke on this."

Sebastian closes his eyes and winces. He wanted enemies. I'm giving him enemies. The more over the top it is, the more fans gag for it, right?

"All right," he says, turning off the camera. "I think that's good."

Sebastian and Christian start moving equipment out to the pool deck where Bellamy will film his interview. We don't follow right away, and instead seek out each other's embrace. Even the simple act of holding each other, touching each other, does something to me. It feels like I'm being rearranged from the inside out, like I'm being torn down and rebuilt into something new. I don't know what the end result will be, but I do know that it will have Bellamy's fingerprints all over it.

———

*Crack.* The sound of billiard balls crashing together, then bouncing away to scatter across the pool table. I straighten from taking the opening shot as the seven drops neatly into the corner pocket. "Solids."

Our first scene is in the basement game room, at the pool table. Bellamy's wearing board shorts and a tank top while I'm decked head to toe in black. Even though we're indoors, he still manages to glow somehow, like the sun is perched on the ceiling, shining down on him.

I'm not entirely okay, like mentally or emotionally. Watching Bellamy do his interview, waiting for Sebastian and Christian to get this scene set up, things are changing and shifting and the ground feels like it's cracking under my feet. I don't know whether a chasm is going to open up beneath me, or whether I'm standing on a mountain about to be formed. The only solid thing I can grab ahold of is Bellamy, but he's not any steadier than I am.

He's standing next to the pool table, feet planted wide, cue braced across the back of his shoulders, showing off the curve of his biceps. He tracks me with a dismissively amused smile as I circle around the table toward him. He's standing in my way, but he doesn't move when I get up in his face. We pause there for a moment, letting Sebastian get a close-up of us, nose-to-nose.

I'm scowling. He's smirking. I'm dark. He's light. I'm an asshole. He's the golden boy. We couldn't be less alike, and yet… and yet, I need him. He's the balm to my rage. He eases the ache in my chest. I can't breathe without him. My heart lurches and falters when he's not around. I don't know when or how it happened, but Bellamy is as pivotal to my existence now as food and water and oxygen.

Bellamy blinks and his smirk disappears, expression softening as he reads what I feel like it's written in black marker on my forehead. He drops a hand from the cue across his shoulders and settles it on my hip. I let my eyes flutter shut at the weight and warmth of it.

"Noel?" Sebastian's voice is tentative and I take a minute to gather myself.

I don't know where all this sentimentality is coming from or why it's chosen this moment to open the flood-gates, but I've got to get my shit together and my ass in gear.

I nod to acknowledge Sebastian's question and when I snap my eyes open, I pin Bellamy with a glare. He lifts his hand from my hip and his lips curl into that smirk again. We're back.

I wedge myself between him and the edge of the table,

then bend over to line up my shot. My ass bumps Bellamy in the groin and I arch my back to make it look good for the camera.

Bellamy smacks me—hard. Even through the thickness of my jeans, the heat of the impact spreads from my ass through to my cock and a shiver runs through me. The shot I take misses by a mile, but that's not the competition I'm angling to win.

I straighten and palm Bellamy's dick through his shorts. "Your turn, asshole."

Bellamy's lips part and his eyes darken. His cock twitches in my hand and he swallows before moving around the table. I make sure I'm standing opposite him, crotch directly in his line of sight. I thrust my hips forward so the camera can see the growing bulge behind the zipper of my jeans.

Bellamy's shot goes wide. He tosses his cue on the table and stalks his way around to me. I lean back, sitting against the ledge of the table, and give Bellamy a once-over as he approaches. "Giving up already?"

"There's another game I'd rather play."

"Oh yeah?"

"Yeah."

Then his mouth is on mine. Hard. Biting. With plenty of tongue and teeth. Lust surges, demolishing every thought that isn't directly related to getting Bellamy naked and under me. My fingers are tangled in his hair so I can hold his head still and ravage his mouth. He moans and sucks on my tongue. The front of my t-shirt is bunched up in his fists.

I shove him away from me and Bellamy stumbles backward. We're both panting, shaking with desire, right on the edge and ready to devour each other at the slightest provocation. I reach for him again, grab him by his tank top, and spin us around so he's bent over, face first, across the top of the pool table. Balls go flying with cracks and thumps. I lay over him, chest against his back, hand on his neck, holding him down.

"You want to play now, fucker?" I growl into his ear.

"Fuck off," Bellamy delivers his line a little too breathy, a little too needy to be believable. It doesn't help that he rubs against me and turns his head to give me access to his throat. Those aren't the actions of someone who's pissed off. They're ones of someone who's begging to get fucked.

I reach around Bellamy and yank on the drawstring of his board shorts, then I tug the elastic waistband down across one hip. He's not wearing anything underneath and I spread my palm against the smooth tanned skin.

"Don't fucking move," I order.

Bellamy makes a half-hearted attempt to shake me off, but when I lever myself up, he stays put. I crouch down, sitting back on my heels, and drag his shorts all the way down his legs. He lifts one foot at a time to kick them off, then spreads his feet wide.

Goddamn. His hole is wrinkled, the skin a couple shades darker than the rest of him. It's nestled between two round, muscled ass cheeks. His balls hang full and heavy, with that thick seam stitched up the middle of his taint. He's beautiful like this, bent over and exposed for me. I want to lick every inch, suck on him until I've left my mark, tease every nerve ending until he's a blubbering mess, then dive into his hole and drive him wild.

With my thumbs, I pry his cheeks farther apart and attack. Bellamy cries when I scrape my teeth hard down his crack and shove my tongue mercilessly into him. I groan involuntarily when I taste him, sunshine and ocean breeze—I'll never get enough of that combination, I'll crave it forever. I eat him out, fuck him with my tongue, sink my teeth into his flesh. When Sebastian tosses me the lube, I slick up my fingers and push three in at the same time. Bellamy screams, but it's only for the camera. He's done his prep and there's no resistance when his muscles give under my intrusion. I don't hesitate to finger fuck him as hard as I can.

"Motherfucker!" He yells at me.

I sneer and force my pinky in too.

"Jesus Christ! Fuck!"

I'd almost believe he was in pain if he wasn't pushing himself back onto my hand, if his ass wasn't trying to suck me in deeper.

"Who's playing now, asshole?" I pull my fingers all the way out, waiting for Sebastian to capture how loose and open Bellamy's hole is. Then I shove all four in again. I find his prostate and hammer on it. I'm relentless, fucking him hard, then grinding on his prostate, again and again until I could probably stick my entire hand in there.

He's sobbing in between his screams. There's a growing puddle of pre-cum on the floor under him. The front of my jeans is wet.

It's time for the next scene.

# CHAPTER
# TWENTY

## BELLAMY

I'm going to be so sore after this shoot and Noel hasn't even gotten his cock into me yet. He definitely won't take it easy on me when he does either. I wince as I push myself up from the pool table.

"Too hard?" Noel gently massages one ass cheek and as absurd as the gesture is, there's something tender and sweet about it.

"No." I meet his gaze and an unspoken message passes between us.

*You're sure?*

*Yes, I'm sure.*

We follow Sebastian and Christian upstairs for the next scene. It's in the big bedroom at the back of the house with the giant windows looking out across the estate. I couldn't believe my eyes when we rolled up to this place earlier and Noel said it belonged to his parents. From the front, the house looks like a castle, complete with windows framed in wrought iron and a big, rustic wooden door. But step inside, and the place expands into a modern open-plan living space. It's like medieval times meets Scandinavian chic.

Sebastian and Christian have taken a padded bench and pushed it up against the window. We'll be fucking in full view of the elaborate in-ground pool, the acres of green grass, and the river and the forest in the distance. I hope some poor hiker out there doesn't try to peer into the house with their binoculars—they'll be getting a show.

Sturdy metal tripods hold up large black boxes that diffuse light across the room. Two cameras have been set up at opposing angles and the third handheld one that Sebastian uses is sitting on the bed. This is technically an amateur operation, but the only real difference between this and the shoot I did for Fetish Studios is the absence of the extra dozen people hovering in the background. Sebastian's managed to create studio-quality production value at a fraction of the cost. No wonder his projected numbers are so good.

"You guys ready?" Sebastian asks, waving me and Noel over. "Noel's going to be 'in charge' in this scene. Bellamy, you can put up a fight and stuff, but he's going to 'win', okay? And make sure you use the bench to hike up your leg."

"Yeah, we got it, boss," Noel says with that mix of derisive fondness that only he could ever pull off.

Sebastian merely shakes his head and grabs his camera.

Noel and I strip all the way down, then I take my position by the window. I can see Noel's reflection in the glass, the darkness of his eyes, the artful muss of his hair, the width of his shoulders, and the glint of his nipple piercing. The connection between us extends into the very core of my being. It's a tether that stretches from my heart to his, and it gets shorter and shorter with each passing day.

I think it's always been there, even when we couldn't stand the sound of each other's names. It's what sent us crashing together, pulling us into orbit in spite of ourselves. And now it's drawing us closer still, with no end in sight.

Christian claps his hands together in front of the camera so Sebastian can line up the video and audio during post-production. Then Sebastian whispers, "Action."

Noel steps up behind me, not touching but close enough to feel his body heat. I tilt my head like I'm glancing over my shoulder at him, and he slams me up against the window. My chest and cheek are smooshed against the glass and I brace myself with my palms. Noel reaches around to grasp my cock and when he gives it a couple jerks, my entire body shudders with pleasure. I half-heartedly try to push away from the window, but he shoves me harder against the glass.

"What do you think you're doing?" he snarls. "You're mine, remember? I'm going to fucking destroy you."

Another shudder runs through me. I am his. In more ways than anyone else knows, than I've even admitted to myself.

"Fuck you," I spit back at him and he responds by yanking my hips out, forcing me to arch my back. The window reflects my image: naked and bent to Noel's will, displayed for all the world to see.

Sebastian moves in and Noel nudges me to the right so we're lined up for the camera. When he lifts his gaze, it collides with mine through the window's reflection. A rightness settles in the deepest part of me, in my heart, in my soul. Me and Noel. Noel and Me. We were always meant to be in each other's lives. We were always meant to end up here.

"What are you waiting for, asshole?" I say, taunting him. "Are you going to fuck me or what?"

Noel's cock notches against my hole, then without any warning, he's fully seated in me.

"Fuck!" I squeeze my eyes shut and breathe through the invasion. I'm completely loose and stretched after his finger fucking downstairs, but his fingers aren't his cock. The sudden, deep penetration punches the air right out of my lungs. My ass is on fire and the flames lick over every inch of my body. Sweat pours from my temples. Every exhale fogs up the window.

Noel doesn't wait for me to adjust. He pulls out almost all the way and rams back in again.

"Fuck!" Oh god, it's so torturously good. Pleasure pounds into me, knocking me sideways, tearing me up. Ecstasy, like a thousand tiny daggers, stabs at me from head to toe. Euphoria wraps around me, tighter and tighter, wringing out mindless bliss from every cell.

My cries echo off the glass, sounding foreign and distant to my ears. Noel lets out a grunt every time he bottoms out. His fingernails dig into my hips and the pain grounds me before I completely fly away.

I'm up on my toes, Noel's thrusts pushing me into the window. The cool glass feels like ice on my throbbing, engorged cock. I'm pumping out so much pre-cum, smearing it all over the glass, that it looks like I might have orgasmed already.

Noel's hand slides down my inner thigh and wraps around the back of my knee. He squeezes and I shift my weight to lift the leg, setting my foot on the padded bench next to us. The change in position gives him greater access, lets him go deeper, fuck me harder. It's all I can do to hang on and let Noel have his way with me.

I burn as he pistons in and out of me. The heat grows and the pressure builds. My balls draw up tight and I curl my toes into the carpet, into the bench cushion, fighting and failing to stave off my orgasm. It's so good. It's so right. And I'm so close.

Noel shutters to a stop all of a sudden and drops his forehead to my shoulder. His breath is hot on my sticky skin. He's still inside me, unmoving but vibrating. He's close to coming too. We're both hovering right on the edge.

"You guys all right? Need a break?" Sebastian asks.

Noel doesn't lift his head when he nods. I reach back for him, fingers threading through his hair. He lifts his chin and our lips meet in a calming, centering kiss. I've never felt so in tune with another person before, like I can read his mind with a simple touch and communicate an essay's worth of thoughts in a single look.

"Okay, let's get a shot of you pulling out, Noel. Then we can move downstairs."

I hiss and wince as Noel eases out of me, then wait for Sebastian's go-ahead before I lower my leg to the floor. My hip and thigh are tight from holding that position for too long and I'm a little unsteady on my feet. But Noel catches me and I cling to him, feeling his heart beat in time with mine.

———

Our last scene is in the great room, in front of the biggest fireplace I've ever laid eyes on. There's already a fire crackling in the grate and the mesh screen in front of it creates flickering shadows on the walls. Christian is changing out the bulbs on the lights to create a warmer, more intimate effect.

"If I can get you guys right here…" Sebastian gestures to a spot in the middle of the rug.

It's some sort of animal skin rug with dark short fur and I really hope it isn't real because we're about to get a lot of bodily fluids on it. I stand on the spot Sebastian pointed at and watch as Noel joins me. His dark hair is damp, his body is all wiry muscles. Light from the fire dances over his skin, catching on the metal of his nipple piercing. My groin tightens at the sight of him. My dick strains toward him.

The moment Sebastian calls out a quiet "Action," Noel and I collide into each other. We're hungry, desperate, and consumed by our need for each other. Noel catches my bottom lip between his teeth. He bites and tugs and I whimper at the delicious pain. I stab my fingers into his hair and yank. He releases my lip and drops his head back, letting me lick my way down his exposed neck, sucking on his Adam's apple, pausing right above his pulse point, then biting his collarbone.

"Fuck," Noel grits out between clenched teeth.

I lash at his nipple piercing with my tongue, flicking it

and pushing it left and right. Noel jolts and his cock jumps when I hook my teeth on the metal bar and pull.

His sweat is salty and dark on my tongue and when I breathe it in, my head spins from intoxication. Dropping to my knees, I lick a trail down the crease of one hip and bury my face in his crotch. How is it possible for anyone to smell so damn good?

Noel threads his fingers through my hair, pushing it back from my face while directing me where to go. He holds me still as he feeds his cock, inch by inch, all the way to the back of my throat until my nose is flush against his pubic bone.

I can't breathe, but then, I don't need to breathe, not when Noel's cock is in my mouth. He keeps me there for long seconds, until my lungs burn, my vision goes dark around the edges, and I start making gurgling choking sounds. When he pulls me off, a rush of spit spills down my chin and a single strand stretches from my lip to the tip of his cock. He only gives me a second to suck in some oxygen before he's in my throat again.

He's fucking my throat and I'm gagging on his cock. Just like he said I would.

I hold onto his thighs and relax my jaw, letting him use my mouth however he likes. My eyes are trained on his face and he's entirely focused on me. The only things that exist are his cock between my lips, his hand in my hair, and his thick quads under my palms. It's almost meditative, my quick little breaths supplying me with just enough air to take me to nirvana.

His legs start to quiver. His rhythm falters. He's already been leaking a steady stream of pre-cum onto my tongue. When he finally pushes me away, I fall onto my heels, chest heaving, head spinning, and skin tingling.

Noel joins me on the rug, pushing me onto my back and straddling my hips. He takes my cock in his hand and my entire body lights up as he gives me a tight, twisting jerk.

"Fuck." My voice is gravelly from all the throat-fucking.

He smirks and does it again. My hips lift off the floor to chase the pleasure and Noel speeds up until he's brought me right to the brink.

"Fuck, wait, stop." I dig my fingers into the rug. I reach to sink my nails into Noel's leg.

He doesn't stop though, shuffling forward, instead, to line my cock up with his hole. Without missing a beat, he lowers himself onto my shaft.

"Oh god, oh fuck, oh Christ."

He's tight. He's hot. He's so fucking perfect and so fucking right. When he starts moving, it's nothing more than little circular motions with his hips. Anything more and I'll shoot my load right into him.

His cock is a steel rod where it lays on my stomach, the head engorged and angry red. The veins running down the length are thick and pulsing. He hisses when I wrap my fingers around it and he grabs my wrist when I try to jerk him.

Oh, yeah, he's just as close as I am. Maybe closer.

I surge off the floor and flip us, pinning him down with my weight. I slant my mouth across his, soft and gentle at first, then rougher, harder. He groans into the kiss. His legs come up around my waist, ankles locking behind my back.

His arms loop around my shoulders and he scores his nails over my shoulder blades.

I'm in him to the hilt, dick pulsing. He clenches around me, sending shivers up my spine.

He tears himself away from our kiss and growls, "Are you going to fuck me or what?"

I grin at his darkening expression. "Don't worry. I'm going to fuck you."

# CHAPTER
# TWENTY-ONE

## NOEL

I should've known Bellamy would pull something like this. It's just like him to take the definition of "hate fuck" and turn it completely on its head. I went at him like a battering ram earlier and now he's exacting his revenge by taking me apart with tenderness.

He rakes his fingers down my chest and stomach, marking bright trails of heat as he sits back on his heels. My legs fall over his thighs, leaving me with no leverage, exposed and vulnerable to Bellamy's devious whims. He's still buried inside me, long and hard, spearing me open, and he takes my aching cock with one hand.

Then he fucks me as devastatingly as I fucked him. Except his version is slow and sweet, rocking his hips up an inch and dropping back down. Goosebumps ripple across my body at the tiny sparks he ignites with his easy, lazy thrusts. His hand moves slowly on my dick, tight enough to make me tremble, but not nearly enough to do anything else.

I'm suspended in this unbearable current of steady, unrelenting comfort. I grasp at the rug beneath me, I writhe, anything to urge him on. I curse out loud when all I can do is lay there and take every single thing Bellamy showers on me.

Attentiveness. Affection. Warmth. Caring.

All of it cranked up past max until I can't contain it anymore.

"Fucking bastard!" I yell as Bellamy keeps up his languid, unhurried rhythm. Pleasure inches through me, gradually lighting up every corner of my body. It dances over my skin and makes me tingle all over. It winds its way into the little crevices of my soul, into places that no one has touched before, that I didn't even know existed, and it makes me feel. So goddamn much.

With one thumb, he twirls circles around the engorged, sensitive head of my dick. With the other, he rubs over my aching taint, flicking at my piercing. His dick slides into me, making itself at home like it belongs there. Like my ass was made for him.

I clamp down, loving how he stretches me wide, how he hits me deep. I try to keep him inside me, filling me up, completing me. Every time he pulls out, I feel the loss like someone's stolen the air out of my lungs. Every time he drives back in, I'm flooded with another burst of ecstasy. His cock, brushing over my prostate, brings tears to my eyes. It's so unbelievably, staggeringly good.

"Bellamy!" I sob, not caring how I sound to the camera or anyone who might watch this later.

I need him on me, holding me, kissing me. I need the closeness, the touch, the intimacy. I reach for him, fingers scrabbling, dragging him up to me. He leans forward and covers my body with his. He slides his hands under my armpits and grips my shoulders, trapping me under him. Still, he moves irritatingly slow.

"Bellamy, please!"

"Shh," he whispers in my ear before trailing delicate kisses across my jaw. He peppers them over my cheeks, my forehead, on both eyes, and down my nose. He teases me with those kisses, snatching them away when I try to capture his mouth with my own.

Tears leak out of the corners of my eyes and run down my temples. My cock burns where it rubs against his stomach. My balls feel bruised with how full and sensitive they are. I don't know how much more of this gentle loving I can take.

Bellamy shifts and his cock punches hard on my prostate. A bolt of lightning careens through me and I let out a shout. "Fuck! Yes! Right there!"

He pulls out halfway and snaps his hips forward, hitting me right on the sweet spot. Tears of relief and gratitude join the ones I shed before. Finally. Finally!

I cling to him as he picks up speed, hammering on my prostate again and again. His balls slap against my ass and his ragged breath huffs in my ear. The scent of sunshine and ocean breeze mixes with the musky aroma of our sex. Light from the fireplace flickers over our skin.

I'm so close to my orgasm. I can practically taste it at the back of my tongue. But no matter how much I strain for it, Bellamy keeps me balanced right on the edge. In desperation, I sink my teeth into the round muscle of his shoulder.

"Fuck! Goddamn it." His rhythm stutters before he picks it up again, faster and harder this time. He lets out a roar in a voice made rough from our sex. His face is buried in the crook of my neck. He squeezes me, so tight I can't breathe, and then he comes.

Bellamy goes taut as his cock swells and twitches inside me. Liquid heat gushes into my channel, searing and molten, marking me as his. It's a delicious feeling, being flooded with his cum. It brings me so close to the brink, almost there, but not quite. Bellamy shudders and stops, leaving me hanging on a thread.

He pulls out instead, and I'm a quivering mess as he extracts himself from my arms. I'm wet and sticky and I want to keep his cum inside me. But when he bends forward to lick over my hole, I can't help but bear down. His cum oozes out, dirty and degrading, and he's right there to catch every drop of it on his tongue. He feeds it to me then goes digging in my hole for more. When I'm finally empty and clean, we keep kissing, trading the last of his cum back and forth until there's nothing left.

"Bellamy, please," I beg him. I haven't come yet and I'm about to expire. I only need one tiny nudge—his hand, his mouth, anything.

But he doesn't give it to me. Not yet. He takes his time revisiting my nipple piercing, my belly button, the sharp points of my hips. He plants kisses along my inner thighs and leaves hickeys in his wake.

"Noel," he says with his fingers poised on my abused hole, waiting for me to make eye contact. We stare into each other's eyes as he pushes back into me, inch by excruciatingly slow inch. His fingers wriggle around until he finds my prostate again. A single tap makes my cock jump on my stomach.

"Please," I plead. I need this to end. Now. Immediately.

Bellamy quirks a grin at me, like it's such a shame I find myself in this predicament. "Please what?"

God, he's the fucking devil. "You motherfucker, you know what!"

His fingers tap on that magic spot, sending electric shocks zinging through me. "That's no way to talk to the only person who can give you what you want."

"Fuck you," I grit out between my teeth. If he isn't going to make me come, then I'll do it myself. I reach for my cock, but he bats my hand out of the way.

"Oh, no. You're not taking this from me." His grin turns evil and conniving and that's the only warning I get before he dives down, taking me right to the back of his throat.

One swallow, one tug on my guiche, one rub on my prostate and that's all it takes. I come, throwing my head back as I shatter. Stars in my eyes and ringing in my ears. My body bows and my balls contract like they're turning inside out. Cum rockets out of my cock. I've never come so hard and for so long in my life.

My jizz paints Bellamy's face. I don't realize until many moments later when I finally manage to open my eyes. He's next to me, covered in my cum, grinning from ear to ear. I drag him down and lick him clean, his lips, his cheeks, his nose, his forehead. I scoop up the white creamy spend and feed it to him like he fed his to me.

"Jesus Christ," someone whispers.

"I know, right? I should've thought of this ages ago."

"They're hotter than we are."

"Hey now, let's not get carried away."

Sebastian and Christian murmur softly in the background as Bellamy and I catch our breaths. I'm drained, spent, and completely undone. My muscles have turned to liquid and my bones have melted into goo. Bellamy's heavy on me, but I don't have the strength to push him off. Not that I want to. I like him exactly where he is, where I can see his face and hear his voice and smell that goddamn sunshine.

Pressure builds in my chest, pulsing and aching, growing stronger with each passing moment. It almost feels like a heart attack, but I think it's a different sort of attack on the heart altogether. I think… this is love.

The second the word materializes in my mind, I know without a single shred of doubt that it's true. I love this man. Deeply and profoundly. No holds barred and undeniable. I love him so much it fucking hurts.

"What is it?" Bellamy asks, voice low and in my ear.

"I didn't say anything."

"I can hear you thinking."

"Then what am I thinking?"

Bellamy snorts at my deliberate obtuseness and rolls to the side. I roll with him, tucking my face into his neck while keeping our limbs tangled together. I'm not ready to face the real world yet. I want to stay with him in our naked little bubble, riding our orgasmic highs.

"You two all right?"

Ugh. Fucking Sebastian.

Bellamy must really be able to hear my thoughts because he chuckles and rubs my back like I'm a petulant toddler who needs soothing. "Yeah, just need a minute."

Then he presses a soft kiss to my temple, and just like that, my mounting irritation disappears. I hug him a little tighter and the pressure in my chest builds a little more.

I don't know what this means or what I should do

about it. Should I tell him I love him? I don't even know if I *want* to be in love with Bellamy. I've never felt this way about anyone before, this soul-deep, indispensable need. It's as if all my vital bodily functions can only operate when I'm near him. I want to pull him inside me and keep him with me forever.

Should I be freaking out about this? I feel like I should be freaking out. That's what people do when they realize they're in love for the first time, right? But there are no red flags waving in the wind or alarm bells ringing through the air. Just this growing ache in my chest that only Bellamy can ease.

I'm not sure what happens now. With us or the video. With anything. I don't know who we are to one another or what direction we want to take from here. I don't know how the video will turn out or what kind of side effects it'll have when it drops. The future is a big black hole and the only thing I know for certain is that we're hurtling toward it with no way to slow down.

Bellamy takes a deep breath and lets it out in a long, slow sigh. Maybe I can read his mind too, because I feel that sigh in the very marrow of my bones.

# TWENTY-TWO

## BELLAMY

I pause in front of my building and balance against the wall to work through some post-run stretches. It's still early, with the air crisp and cool, and I have the street to myself. This is usually my favorite time of day and I'm usually elated after a solid morning run.

Except my pace was pathetic and I turned around before reaching the midway point. All I want to do is go upstairs and crawl back into bed. I've been doing that a lot lately, curling up at all hours with my phone held close to my chest. I've been clinging to it like it's a lifeline, my only connection to the one person who's constantly on my mind.

I heave a sigh and let myself into the building. I really hope Santino's still asleep so I can mope around the kitchen by myself. But the second I push open our apartment door, he's right there, ready to accost me.

"Dude, what the fuck is this?" He holds up his phone and I squint at it.

Before I can make out what he's trying to show me, he pulls the phone away.

"You made a video with Noel Carrington?"

Right. That. The video dropped at midnight and I had to turn off my notifications so my phone wouldn't burn up while I tried to sleep. "Tried" being the operative word. I haven't been very successful on that front lately.

I manage a sheepish smile. "Yeah, I did."

"And you didn't fucking tell me?" His eyes bulge out of his head.

I shrug and grab the water pitcher from the fridge. "We put out teasers." Well, Noel did, as a member of The Camboy Network. I kept my social media silent to keep the collaboration a surprise.

"No, you didn't! Not to me! I'm your roommate!" Santino paces across the living room, then back toward me. "Have you seen these comments?"

I haven't. I'm a little afraid of the reception it'll get. I mean, I know Sebastian is great at what he does and everyone loves a good hate fuck. But I've seen the rough cuts and it's… a lot. It's hate fucking twisted around and perverted until it's something else entirely. The connection between me and Noel comes through like a punch in the jaw. There's a level of intimacy that you wouldn't normally associate with enemies or rivals, or even performers pretending to be enemies or rivals. It's blatantly obvious to me that we're lovers, but Noel and Sebastian have both assured me no one else will notice. I have no choice but to trust them.

"They're wild!" Santino starts reading them off while I collapse on the couch.

*OMG, that's so hot!!!*

*My dick hurts from how many times I've jacked off to this!!*

*Noel's an asshole. Team Bellamy forever!!*

*Are they going to make another one? Please say yes!*

*Team Noel all the waaayyy!!! Destroy that ass!!!*

*They really do hate each other!!!*

My heart rate had easily settled to resting after my half-hearted run, but now it's creeping back up. The fans seem to like the video. It sounds like they're buying the story we're trying to sell. For some reason, that makes me more nervous than I already was.

There's so much of me and Noel in that video, and the thing is, I don't even understand what most of it is. It's so raw and unfiltered, so gritty and unrefined. It's pure, unadulterated emotion pouring out of us—emotions I haven't come to terms with myself.

And it's not like Noel and I have *talked* about it or anything. Because that would be the mature, adult thing to do. We spent the rest of the weekend at his parents' ridiculously extravagant house with Sebastian and Christian. We cooked—well, Christian did most of the cooking—, played board games, cuddled in front of the fire, cuddled in bed, cuddled when we woke up in the morning all wrapped up in each other. It was downright idyllic. Neither of us wanted to ruin that stretch of simplicity, knowing that things could get complicated once the video dropped.

"Jesus! People are getting dirty! Team Bellamy versus Team Noel. There's going to be a riot in the streets!" Santino bounces on his feet. "Oh shit, listen to this. 'Does anyone think they might actually like each other?' What?!"

I fling my arm over my eyes. This type of stuff isn't supposed to bother me. Fans and media say all kinds of shit all the time and I never so much as flinch. But this is different… everything about this collab is different.

Or maybe something about me has changed.

"Dude, you okay? You look like shit."

I open my eyes to find Santino standing above me, phone forgotten as he regards me with a concerned expression.

"Yeah, I'm fine." I don't convince either of us.

"Are you sure? Because you've been in a weird funk lately. Ever since you came back from that New York trip." He glances at his phone, then back at me. "Oh shit, is that when you filmed the video?"

"Yeah."

"Oh shit." He sits down on the coffee table. "How was it? Was it like… ahrr!" He curls his fingers into claws and mimics what I think is supposed to be me and Noel going at each other.

Santino doesn't know about me and Noel, that there *is* a "me and Noel." And suddenly, the urge to tell him is so intense that the words spill out of my mouth before I can stop them.

"We're actually together, sort of. I mean, we're not, you know, yeah."

*Real eloquent, Bell.*

Santino's understandably confused. "What?"

I sigh and rub the heels of my hands into my eyes. "It started at the convention in Vegas. Remember that?"

Santino nods. "Yeah, that was right after your edging video."

"That's the one. We, uh, hooked up and then…"

When I dare to peek at Santino, his jaw is on the floor. I wait for him to say something, to ask me if I'm joking or to jump to his feet and freak out. But he just sits there, stunned.

"Um, you okay?"

He shakes his head and blinks to clear away the shock. "Yeah, I just… holy shit, you and Noel Carrington?"

"Yup."

"That's… but you hate each other!"

I wince. "We got over it?"

He drops his gaze to his phone. "Jesus. No wonder the video is so hot."

"You can't tell anybody," I warn, sitting up to show him how serious I am.

"Of course!" Santino raises his hands, palms out. "No one'll find out anything from me." But then he leans in and lowers his voice. "So, uh, how was it really? Is he good at fucking? I bet he's really good, isn't he?"

I haven't smiled in days, so the grin tugging on my lips feels stilted. "Yeah, he's really good."

"Fucking A. I'd go for that dick." Santino leans back with his hands behind him. "So what, you guys are like, boyfriends now, or something?"

"Or something," I mutter. It's as good a label as anything at this point.

Santino nods. "Cool cool. I've gotta say, I'm not that surprised."

I cock an eyebrow. "You're not?"

He shrugs as he stands. "Naw, man. I mean, chemistry is chemistry, right?" He saunters off to his room without waiting for a response.

I guess he is right. Noel and I have always been explosive together—the difference between exploding at each other and exploding with each other is merely a matter of perspective.

My phone buzzes where it's still strapped to my arm and I scramble to pull it out of the protective case. My heart lifts at Noel's face filling my screen and I jab at the *Accept* button so hard, I kind of hurt my finger. "Hey!"

"Hey." The phone is in his hand, pointed upward so the camera captures his bare chest and shoulders. His hair is wet.

"Did you just get out of the shower?"

He smolders into the camera. "Yeah."

My cock twitches as I picture him naked, water sluicing over his skin. My breath catches in my chest and my vision goes a little hazy.

Noel chuckles, the sound going straight to my groin. "Are you imagining me in the shower?"

"Maybe."

He turns his smolder up to eleven and disappears from the screen for a moment. When he comes back, he's on his bed, arm tucked up behind his head. "You're so slutty for me."

I school my face into a bored expression. "I just like shower scenes."

"Oh yeah? So this doesn't do it for you?" He pans the camera down his body, the glint of his nipple piercing, the water droplets collecting between his pecs, the ridges and valleys of his abs, his semi-hard cock lying on his stomach.

Yeah, that fucking does it for me. I squeeze myself through my running shorts. God, I want to lick up every stray drop of water on his skin. I want to wrap my lips around his dick and feel it grow and stiffen on my tongue. I want him so viscerally that my heart hurts from not touching him.

"Hey, so, Sebastian says the video's doing well." Noel's tone has lost that teasing edge.

"Awesome." I cringe at how unawesome I sound. I should be ecstatic. The video is doing exactly what we hoped it would do. Go viral, boost subscriber numbers, and make bank. But I don't feel the comforting satisfaction that comes with knowing my account is getting a nice juicy bump.

Noel turns to his side, his face half obscured by the pillow. He looks as miserable as I feel. "I miss you," he whispers.

Fuck if his admission doesn't make my heart hurt even more. "I miss you too."

"Are you sure you won't let me fly you out to New York?"

This isn't the first time he's brought it up, and as much as I'd love to bum a flight off Noel, I can't in good conscience use him like that. "I'm sure."

"What if I fly out to you?"

I roll my eyes. "That's the same thing."

"No, it's not."

"Noel." I try to sound assertive, but it comes out pleading. It's hard enough saying no to him when everything inside me aches from being so far away. It won't take much for me to break if he keeps going on like this.

"Okay, fine. But if you change your mind…"

"I know, I know."

A beat passes before Noel speaks again. "We haven't missed anything have we? I'll be in Philly, then Miami. And you'll be New York while I'm in Miami, and then in Chicago when I get back to New York. Which means we won't see each other until the Grabby's in two months."

When he puts it that way, those eight weeks feel like forever. Am I letting my pride get in the way? Maybe I should take Noel up on his offer so I'll stop feeling like I'm dying a little every day.

"It's not that long," I force myself to say.

Noel looks off camera when he speaks. "Yeah, sure, if you say so."

His words slice through me, leaving my insides spilling out onto the floor. "Noel, please."

He turns back to the camera again, eyes swirling with emotions he's plucked straight from my heart. "Two months." He tries for a smile that doesn't reach his eyes. "It's not that long."

## CHAPTER
# TWENTY-THREE

**NOEL**

Two months is really fucking long. And the twelve hours we've had to get reacquainted is not nearly enough. I want to keep Bellamy naked and in bed for at least another forty-eight. Hell, if I had things my way, he'd be on a plane back to New York with me after the Grabby Awards. I still haven't ruled out the possibility—I'm not above a bit of kidnapping.

We got ready together in our hotel suite earlier. It's so easy being in the same space with him, a casual hand across the waist, dropping a kiss on a naked shoulder. I feel so much calmer and more carefree when I'm with him. I never realized how much rigid tension I carry around until I started spending time with Bellamy and it all melted away. The relief when I stepped into his arms again last night was so immense I almost dropped to my knees. I need him, not only for sex or the stinging banter, but to feel whole.

Out of necessity, we take separate cars to the awards

ceremony since no one knows about our relationship. Putting on our personas to walk the red carpet feels a bit like going undercover, sneaking covert glances at each other while pretending we're still enemies. We've come a long way since Las Vegas, but some things will never change—we'll always be good at knocking each other down a peg.

"Noel! What was it like to finally work with your arch-nemesis?"

I shrug and glower. "Anti-climactic. He's just as pathetic as I thought he would be."

"Noel! You and Bellamy have been rivals for most of your careers. Why did you agree to the collaboration?"

I purse my lips in smug satisfaction. "I wouldn't call it a collaboration. More like a confrontation."

"Who won?"

I scoff. "If you have to ask that question, you clearly haven't watched the video closely enough."

"Noel! Will you be reuniting for a sequel?"

I never answer that question. I smolder straight into the camera, then turn and walk away. It's fun slipping back into this role, especially when everyone eats it up. But it doesn't give me the same kick of excitement anymore; I'd rather curl up with Bellamy instead.

Sitting through the first half of the show on opposite sides of the ballroom is pure torture. My instincts keep telling me to march across the room and scoop him up. Sebastian has to change seats with me so I stop gazing at Bellamy with hearts in my eyes, but that doesn't prevent me from looking over my shoulder to reassure myself he's still there. Every time I do, he's watching me with that arrogant, self-assured smirk. The same one that used to taunt me to no end. The same one I still want to kiss right off his face.

When I step into the darkened backstage, I have to restrain myself from running to Bellamy and inserting myself into his arms. It's only been a few hours since I touched him, but my fingers are already itching to feel the warmth of his skin, the roughness of his stubble, and the silkiness of his hair.

He's wearing this sexy as fuck plum-colored crushed velvet suit that's perfectly tailored to his shoulders and follows the line of his torso down to his trim hips. The white shirt he's wearing underneath is open at the collar, revealing just enough skin to tantalize and tease. There's a matching white carnation tucked into his breast pocket.

Bellamy meets my gaze and a silent understanding passes between us. His shoulders drop an inch, like he can relax now that we're together. His lips twitch and I narrow my eyes for whatever snarky comment he's got coming.

"How many peacocks did you kill for your outfit?" he says, loud enough for the stage manager standing next to us to hear.

I roll my eyes and fight to keep the smile off my face. The bastard knows the feathers are fake. "More than you could ever afford."

He cocks an eyebrow. "Haven't you heard? I'm rich now, thanks to how thoroughly I owned your ass."

"You mean how thoroughly I wrecked yours."

Bellamy lowers his chin to his chest and covers his mouth to smother a chuckle. Then he swoops down to pick something off the floor. "Dropped this."

He's holding a feather from my outfit, an all-black ensemble inspired by Billy Porter, crowned by a tuxedo jacket with a plume of feathers in place of traditional tails. I try to snatch it from him, but Bellamy jerks his hand away and sticks the feather behind his ear. My breath catches in my chest. To everyone else, it'll look like a flag he's stolen from me. But to us, it's a silent token that he's mine.

The stage manager glances from me to the feather behind Bellamy's ear, confusion written across his face. But then he shrugs and gives us our cue. Bellamy bows exaggeratedly, allowing me to proceed before him. I flash him the middle finger as I stride out onto the stage, giddiness and adrenaline bubbling in my veins.

The audience goes wild at the sight of us. People are on their feet. The shouting goes on for minutes while we bask in their adoration and praise. I peek at Bellamy and he's glowing, as always, like the sunshine has broken through the ceiling and made a spotlight especially for him.

He turns to catch my gaze and electricity arcs between us, sparking so bright that the audience erupts again. I smirk, puffing out my chest. Bellamy's eyes crinkle at the edges as he cranks his smile up a few more watts. It takes another full minute for everyone to settle.

"We're here to present the award for Best Flip Fuck," I read from the teleprompter. Our collab wasn't released in time for this year's show, but the award organizers were so desperate to get us on stage that they booted the original presenters for us instead.

"Because, you know, we've got some experience with that." Bellamy licks his lips and gives me a once-over.

I shoot a haughty look back at him. He cocks his head and edges into my personal space. The scent of sunshine envelops me.

"Oh, come on," he says, going off-script. He palms his crotch, the movement exaggerated for the audience's bene-fit. "We all know how much you liked it." They whoop and holler as he leans in, his nose ghosting over my cheek.

Fucker wants to play, huh? I know how to play.

I slap his hand away and jam my palm against his erec-tion, squeezing hard enough that he comes up on his toes. His jaw drops open in a quiet gasp and his pupils dilate with lust.

"Not as much as *you* liked it." I pitch my voice low and Bellamy shudders in response.

We're so close, nose-to-nose, glaring at each other the way everyone loves. A simple tilt of my head would bring my lips to Bellamy's, and I could attack him with my mouth the way everyone wants. Bellamy's eyes narrow, throwing down the challenge, daring me to do it.

A roar fills my ears when we make contact, hard and aggressive, both of us fighting for dominance as our tongues and teeth clash together. I get a hold of his bottom lip, sink my teeth into it, and tug. The whimper Bellamy lets out is loud enough for the microphone to pick up, and just like that, we've incited chaos, with people climbing on chairs and tables, and every phone in the room trained on us.

Bellamy pushes me away so forcefully that I don't fake my stumble. His eyes flash with defiance. "You son of a bitch."

I wipe my mouth with the back of my hand. "Mother-fucker," I spit back at him.

It takes god knows how long for the audience to finally calm down and we manage to read out the nominees without another incident. Bellamy opens the envelope. We hand over some awards. I don't even register who wins. All I can think about is getting Bellamy backstage, finding a secluded spot, and getting my tongue down his throat again.

Bellamy follows me off stage and I drag him into a supply closet. I shove him against the door and ram my thigh between his legs, pressing hard enough that he gasps.

"Fuck." He grinds himself on me. "I can't believe you did that on stage."

"You started it." I rake my teeth down Bellamy's neck.

His fingers tighten in my hair. "Noel."

Goddamn. When Bellamy says my name like that, full of desperation and need that only I can sate... it does something unholy to me. I slant my mouth over his and surrender to the arousal that thrums through me whenever I'm with him.

My hands drop to Bellamy's belt and two seconds later, I'm down on my knees with his dick in my palm. My poor tuxedo trousers will have to forgive me. Bellamy is hard and leaking and so fucking gorgeous that my mouth waters at the sight. I swirl my tongue around the smooth, swollen glans and Bellamy bites back a cry. His hips cant forward and I let him push inch after inch past my lips.

My eyes drift shut as I descend to a place that's simultaneously heaven and hell. Bellamy's taste is on my tongue, his scent is in my nose. I want to lose myself in him, but a voice at the back of my head reminds me that Bellamy's plane ticket still says San Francisco, not New York. This time we have together will come to an end, whether I like it or not.

I suck and swallow, desperate to erase any thought that

isn't from here and now. I jam his cock down my throat until my nose is pressed right into his pelvic bone. I wiggle my tongue along the underside of his length, bury the tip into his slit. Above me, Bellamy whines and whimpers, curls falling over his forehead as he watches me blow him.

I want his cum. I want to take his essence and gorge myself on it. I want a stomach full of him so that when I walk away, at least I have a part of him inside me. Sunshine and ocean breeze, in me and around me, forever.

"Noel." Bellamy's knees shake and he bangs his head against the door. "I'm coming. Fuck, I'm coming."

He floods my mouth and I drink down every last drop. Even when he goes soft between my lips, I'm not ready to let him go. I hold him in my mouth, petting him with my tongue, waiting until Bellamy finally drags me to my feet.

He kisses me, licking into my mouth, seeking out anything I haven't swallowed. I'm raging for him, my cock eager for its turn. I rub myself on him, hands kneading his ass to pull him closer.

Something vibrates against my hand—Bellamy's phone. We ignore it, but it doesn't stop.

"Fuck, sorry." Bellamy breaks our kiss, chest heaving with each breath, lips bruised and wet from our kisses. He pulls his phone out of his back pocket and the screen's light illuminates his expression as it turns into a frown.

My heart plummets and dread rushes in. Nothing good will come from this call and I'll lose what little time we have left.

Bellamy swipes his thumb over the screen and brings the phone to his ear. "Hello? Mom?"

# CHAPTER
# TWENTY-FOUR

## BELLAMY

"Hi, dear…"

It's loud in the background, with an echoing PA system and lots of commotion.

"Mom? Where are you?"

"Uh, at the hospital."

"What?" I grab the hem of my pants that are still down around my thighs.

Noel's hands cover my own and he efficiently tucks me in and zips me up like he's one of those old-school butlers or grooms or whatever.

"We had to—hold on a moment." There's a muffled sound like she's covering the phone with her hand.

"What's going on?" Noel whispers to me, but I shake my head. I'd also like to know what the fuck is going on.

Mom comes back and sighs into the phone. "They're moving him to the respiratory care unit and keeping him overnight." She's huffing and puffing like she's been running.

"Mom, what happened?" I nearly shout into the phone as my mind spirals to the worst-case scenarios. Dad collapsed. He had a heart attack. He's dying.

"Here, give me that." There's a fumble and then Twyla comes on the line. "Hello? Bell?"

Thank god Mom's not alone. "Yeah, what's happening?"

"Dad couldn't breathe so we had to call an ambulance. He's got pulmonary edema."

"He's got what?"

Twyla heaves a sigh. "Fluid in his lungs."

Fluid in the lungs sounds like it might be one of those worst-case scenarios. "How the hell did that happen?"

"How the fuck do I know?" Twyla hisses into the phone. "No, Mom, it's on the third floor." An elevator dings. "I don't know. They've got him on oxygen and gave him a bunch of meds. There's like a hundred different tests they want to run." Twyla's voice is harder than I'm used to hearing. She's had to grow up a lot in the last couple years.

"Fuck. Okay, I'm coming home."

There's a slight hesitation on Twyla's end. "Are you sure?"

Noel's frowning into his phone, brow furrowed in determination. Despite the blowjob he gave me, his make-up hasn't budged. Dark eyeliner and even darker mascara frame his eyes and his lipstick is still perfectly lined. I've only just gotten Noel back in my arms and we were supposed to have another night together. I haven't gotten my fill of him yet. I need more of his hands on my body, his lips on my skin. I need to be inside him and feel him contract around me.

This isn't enough. We haven't had enough.

But Dad. And Mom and Twyla. They need me. What if something happens while I'm getting a cock shoved up my ass? What if there's a life-or-death decision and I'm not there to help make it?

"There's a flight leaving in an hour. I can get you on it if you leave now." Noel doesn't look up when he speaks. There's no question in his voice. No indecision or uncertainty. Just action, sure and confident and bold. When I don't respond, he raises an eyebrow in question.

"Bell?" I can tell Twyla's trying to keep her voice steady, but there's an unmistakable note of hope in it, like she wants me to be there but doesn't know if it's okay to ask.

"No, tell him he doesn't need to come. He's so busy. We'll handle things." Mom's words in the background solidifies my decision.

"I'm coming."

Noel gives me a single nod and his thumbs start flying over his phone. I open the closet door and we make a beeline for the exit.

"Text me what room Dad's in," I say to Twyla. "I'll let you know my ETA when I have it."

"You're not going to have time to get your things from our suite." Noel's by my side as we jog toward the hotel's main entrance.

Heads swivel when we rush by and spectators share wide-eyed expressions with their friends. If I was paying more attention, I probably would've heard them whispering about me and Noel and why the hell we're running through the hotel together.

There's a line of cabs half a block down and when the

hotel valet sees us approaching, he waves the first car over.

"Your ticket confirmation is on your phone," Noel says. "Check in while you're on the road. Just buy whatever you need when you land. I'll take care of your stuff here."

I stand with one foot in the backseat of the cab and one foot on the sidewalk. It hits me, all of a sudden, how incredible Noel is being right now. Not a trace of selfishness or arrogance or entitlement—all the things I've accused him of before. His focus is entirely on me and what I need.

I grab his face and haul him to me, planting a firm kiss on his lips. It lasts for only a second before he pushes me away.

"Go," he says, eyes twinkling and mouth curled into a smile, then he shoves me into the car.

The door slams shut before I can say anything else and the driver pulls away from the curb. I stare at the image of Noel growing smaller and smaller in the side mirror while he stands there, watching the cab drive away.

I don't realize Noel booked me a first-class ticket until I get on the damn plane. I mean, it's not a huge plane, so the difference between first class and economy is about five feet of space. But that distance means a steady top-up of my beer. It's a good distraction from all the what-ifs flying through my mind.

*What if I can't find a taxi when I land? What if I can't find them in the hospital? What if Dad gets worse while I'm thirty-thousand feet in the air? What if I get there too late?*

The only thing that truly calms me is the thought of Noel. His steady matter-of-factness. The clear and direct instructions he gave me. The knowledge that he's only a phone call away and he'll always know what to do. He's my anchor in all this chaos, even if he's miles away.

My phone is in my hand the second the wheels touch the tarmac. There are dozens of notifications waiting for me, but I don't have time to glance at them. I pull up Twyla's text to double-check the hospital name and Dad's room number. Then I stuff my phone in my pocket and race to get out of the airport.

I get to the hospital in record time and find Dad's room without too much trouble. Mom's sprawled on an old vinyl-upholstered recliner and Twyla is perched on the narrow window ledge. The other bed in the room is empty.

"Mom."

She stands to give me a long, tight hug, and I can feel the tension in her body drain away as I hold her. She wants me here, needs me here, regardless of what she said on the phone earlier. I hug Twyla next, for just as long and just as tightly.

"How's he doing?" I ask.

Dad is unconscious, propped up at an angle, face covered in an oxygen mask, and an IV line coming out of his arm. It's not the first time I've seen him like this, but it still knocks me back a step. When Twyla and I were kids, he was so tall and broad and could lift both of us at the same time, one under each arm. But that was eons ago, so far into the past that it barely seems real.

"He's still not breathing great, but the oxygen is helping." Mom fusses with the bedsheets covering him. "They've given him medication to help drain his lungs."

"How long does that take? Do they know what caused it in the first place?"

Mom shakes her head, lips pressed in a firm line. "I don't know. No one knows."

"I thought you said they were running a bunch of tests," I say to Twyla.

"They did. They are. They said it might be a pulmonary embolism, but they can't find the blood clot. It might not even be there anymore. Blood clots can dissolve on their own." She climbs back onto her perch by the window.

I hate that she knows all these fancy medical terms, that she's felt the need to read up on it and learn what they mean. Teenagers shouldn't have to become amateur doctors because they have a sick parent. They should be playing volleyball, getting into trouble after school, and fooling around with other teenagers.

"So, now what?" I ask, turning back to Dad.

"Wait and see," Mom says, giving me a sad smile that's more discouraging than anything else.

That's the thing about caring for loved ones who are sick. There's so much waiting around, not being able to do anything, uncertain about what's going to happen in the end. All we can do is sit there, hoping for the best and knowing it might not be enough.

"Why don't you two go home?" I say. It's pushing midnight and they've already been at the hospital for hours. "I'll stay with Dad and you can come back in the morning."

"No, that's okay, dear. You don't need to do that." Mom reaches for her purse and fishes out her car keys. "You can take Twyla home."

I take the keys but hold them out to Twyla. "Mom,

please. Go home. Get some rest." I give Twyla a pointed look and she nods in understanding.

"Come on, Mom." She hops down from the ledge and takes Mom's arm.

"Thank you, dear. You're the sweetest. What would we do without you?" She kisses me on the cheek before they slip quietly out of the room.

*What would we do without you?* She doesn't mean anything by it, and yet I feel the weight of every word as I sink into the recliner by the bed. It's been seven years since I threw myself into camming to help pay the bills. And before that, I was working as many jobs as I could cram into a day. There had never been any other option, and I don't see another option now either.

The reality is Dad's condition can only get worse, not better. He'll need more medical care and more stays in the hospital. Twyla's going away for college next year. There's still a mortgage on the house. The bills never stop rolling in and there's no choice but to keep hustling.

It's exhausting. I'll never admit it to Mom or Dad or even Twyla, but sometimes, it's too much. The fatigue soaks right into my bone marrow, it goes deep into my mind or psyche or whatever, and my brain feels physically tired.

I pull out my phone to send Noel a message and my screen is filled with notifications. Looks like our little act is making the waves we wanted it to. I quickly switch my phone to Do Not Disturb, white-listing Noel, Mom, and Twyla's numbers. Then I type out a quick message for Noel.

BELLAMY

Made it to the hospital. Gonna stay here for the night. Sent Mom and Twyla home.

NOEL

How's your dad?

Asleep. We'll know more in the morning.

You going to an afterparty?

Noel doesn't respond right away. He's probably sitting in a nightclub with a glass of whiskey in hand. He'll have people coming to him—performers, directors, producers—like he's a king on his throne and they're all begging for a few morsels of his attention. I've seen it before, at other parties, and marveled at the arrogance of the man. Now I know that the edgy bad boy persona everyone sees is nothing more than a mask for his soft, squishy insides.

NOEL

Maybe.

BELLAMY

Don't have too much fun without me.

Never. It's not fun when I don't have anyone to glare at.

I chuckle softly under my breath.

BELLAMY

You glare at everyone.

NOEL

But it's only fun when I do it to you.

My heart shouldn't skip a beat at the little zings we can't quite avoid when we talk to each other. And yet, it does. I close my eyes and hold that sharp sting close. I savor the way it needles, the prick of pain that cuts through the sweetness and makes it real.

Pulling the recliner next to the bed, I slip my hand into Dad's. It's a lot thinner than it used to be. The bones feel fragile and the skin is almost translucent. His chest rises and falls unevenly in short, stuttering breaths, and the screen of the heart rate monitor blips faster than normal.

I cross my arms on the bed and lay my head down. I wish Noel were here.

## NOEL

I wait until Bellamy's cab vanishes into the night before turning back toward the hotel, pulling up tomorrow's flight schedule to Cleveland while I go. The earliest flight is really goddamn early, but there's one first-class seat left on it, so it's going to be mine.

Bellamy didn't ask me to follow him to Cleveland and I'm not going to give him the option to shut me down. If we have to give up precious time together now, then I intend on recouping every single hour.

I slip back into the ballroom and quietly find my seat again.

"Everything okay?" Sebastian asks when I sit down.

"Yeah."

He shoots a glance across the room to Bellamy's table. "Where's Bellamy?"

"He had to go."

"Go? Go where?" He backs down when I shoot him a warning look.

Who knows what happens during the rest of the show? All I can think about is Bellamy and mentally tracking his progress to the airport, then through the air, then to the hospital. My eyes are glued to my phone, refreshing the flight status page every five seconds. I only realize the show is over when Sebastian's hand lands on my shoulder.

"Hey, what's going on?" His voice is full of concern and his eyes are full of worry.

The words spill out of my mouth in a rush. "His dad's in the hospital. He had to go."

Sebastian's eyes widen. "Oh, shit."

Christian steps in, holding his phone between us. "You guys need to see this."

I don't understand what I'm seeing at first. It's a social media post, a video. It starts out shaky, like the person had to fumble to get their phone out. Then Bellamy appears on screen, dressed in his purple crushed velvet suit. I'm beside him, peacock feathers flowing behind me. The video follows as we rush past the lucky videographer and out of the main hotel entrance.

My stomach sinks as I read the caption.

*Where are Noel Carrington and Bellamy Blais rushing off to together?!?! #Blaisington*

God-fucking-damn it. This was taken no more than twenty minutes ago. The video already has hundreds of likes.

"There's more." Christian flicks the screen and my stomach falls straight through the floor.

Pictures, dozens of them, like a stop-motion movie of

us at the curb, Bellamy kissing me, me pushing him into the cab. There's even a heavily filtered photo of me standing there watching the car disappear into the distance, matched with Whitney Houston's *I Will Always Love You* playing in the background.

"Fuck."

Sebastian takes my arm. "Um, let's get out of here and regroup."

It's only then that I notice all the eyes on me, the curious frowns, the disbelieving glances at their phones. We're halfway out the room when a reporter comes rushing up to us.

"Noel, what's the nature of your relationship with Bellamy? Where was Bellamy going in that taxi? Was the whole rivalry thing even real?"

Every syllable out of his mouth makes me scowl harder and I would've gone off on the guy if Christian wasn't physically blocking him from me. Rhys and Hayden hurry to catch us and my friends form a protective ring around me as we rush out of the building.

No one says anything on the ride to the hotel where Bellamy and I have our suite. Sebastian's head is bent over his phone the entire time, a crease in his brow as he monitors social media.

"Here." Hayden presses a glass into my hand the minute we're in the safety of the suite.

I don't bother checking what's in it before tossing the entire thing back. I don't taste the whiskey. I don't even feel the burn as it filters down to my stomach.

"Okay, so…" Sebastian trails off with a head tilt. "Do you think Bellamy knows? Should we call him?"

I shake my head. Bellamy's got more important things

to worry about at the moment. "He's probably still in the air. I don't want to bother him with this."

Sebastian gives a single decisive nod. "Got it. In that case, we need to come up with a statement. It doesn't need to be a whole long explanation or anything. Just something to acknowledge the pictures and buy us some time. We could go with the personal emergency angle and ask the public to respect our privacy. Guilt everyone into holding off their questions until we get our story straight."

I've been sitting on the couch, staring unseeingly at the carpet. My mind takes note of the conversation happening around me, but I don't really hear what anyone's saying until someone squeezes my shoulder. Someone else sits next to me, pressing up against my arm. Sebastian crouches down in front of me and puts his hand on my knee.

"Noel?"

I keep replaying that run through the hotel lobby in my head. The bright flash of joy when Bellamy grabbed me and kissed me. I hated having to send him packing, but that kiss felt like a promise. That we weren't done yet. That what we have is real and we're going to make this work somehow.

And now that moment is plastered all over the internet and will probably become a meme by morning. That moment was supposed to be ours. This whole relationship was supposed to be ours to hold and cherish and savor. We never intended for the world to know about us—not anytime soon anyway, and certainly not splashed all over social media like it's some sort of scandal.

My anger starts simmering, eating away at the numbness until it's the only thing I feel. Anger. Fury. Rage. How dare they? How fucking dare they? I should track down every single one of those motherfuckers and sue them until they're destitute and living on the street. Then I'll go after every single person they've ever loved and do the same to them.

I'm on my feet before I know it, pushing past everyone to pace the room. I'll hire a private investigator and dig up every embarrassing, shameful thing they've ever done and dump it all online. I'm going to rip their lives to shreds. I'm going to fucking destroy them.

I'm stopped by a pair of feet standing in my way. Someone grips my arms and gives me a shake.

"Noel!"

I blink and the red clears from my vision just enough for me to make out Sebastian in front of me.

"You're not going to sue anyone. You're not going to destroy anyone. Yes, you were muttering, but we all heard you."

My gaze flicks to Rhys, Hayden, and Christian who are all standing at a distance like they're afraid of getting too close.

"What we are going to do is some savvy public relations. We'll spin this thing and use it to our advantage."

I frown at him. "Our advantage?"

"Yeah!" Sebastian's grin is much too bright for our current predicament. "Don't you see? This is an opportunity! Everyone loves a good enemies-falling-in-love story. That's why the hate fucking works so well!"

I grit my teeth, clench and unclench my fingers a few times. Somewhere in the back of my mind, I know Sebastian's right. But that doesn't mean I have to like it.

"Rhys and Hayden are going out to the afterparties.

They'll play it off like it's no big deal. Christian and I will stay here with you."

"You don't have to do that." I know Sebastian loves the afterparty networking scene.

He gives me another shake. "I do. Don't argue with me." Then he drops his hands and turns to Rhys and Hayden to give them more detailed instructions.

I collapse back onto the couch, wishing Bellamy was here, or that I'd gotten on the plane with him. I wish we could ensconce ourselves away from the world in our own little bubble where everything is happy and bright. Where he doesn't have to worry about his dad's health or his sister's college tuition. Where this charade of a rivalry doesn't exist and our public images are irrelevant.

Christian sits down next to me. "Don't worry," he says in his quiet, self-assured way. "This is going to be a gold mine and Sebastian's going to wring out every ounce of the shiny stuff."

I have no doubt Sebastian can do that. I'd just rather not be the one being wrung.

# CHAPTER
# TWENTY-SIX

## BELLAMY

I'm awoken by something buzzing against my face. I groan and grimace, trying to swat it away, but my hand lands on something solid and rectangular. When I try to lift my head, sharp pain shoots up my back. Fuck.

I've fallen asleep sitting in the recliner, head pillowed on Dad's hospital bed. He's still out cold, although the machine monitoring his heart is beeping a little slower than it did last night. I wince as I stretch the stiffness out of my muscles, then reach for my phone. It's Noel calling and my heart does a flip in my chest.

"Hey," I answer the video call as I ease myself off the recliner and slip out of the room. I need coffee. A lot of it.

"Hey, how's your dad?"

Out of nowhere, my chin starts to wobble and my eyes start to sting. It's not just that he thought to ask, but that it was the first thing he asked about. And now that I'm not in panic mode anymore, all my feelings suddenly have free rein. I hurry toward the exit sign at the end of the hallway and burst through the door into the stairwell.

"Bell?"

I sink down onto the top step, slumping against the concrete wall. The cold seeps through my clothes and cools the riot of emotions inside me.

"Bell? Talk to me."

I aim the camera at myself and cringe at my picture in the top right-hand corner. I am the epitome of death warmed over.

"Jesus, you look like shit."

"Gee, thanks." I cover my face with my hand, then set my elbow on my knee to prop my head up.

"Did you sleep? Have you eaten?"

I peek at my phone through my fingers. "What do you think?"

Noel's not impressed. "I'll have some food delivered to you."

I wrestle with the tears that seem determined to escape my lashes. "You don't have to do that."

"Yes, I do. You can't stop me."

Christ, he's so arrogant and pretentious and I miss him so goddamn much. "In that case, extra coffee, please."

"So much coffee you'll be jittery for days."

That sounds like heaven right now. A persistent little fucker of a tear gathers at the corner of one eye and before I can hide it from Noel, it runs down my cheek.

"Bell—"

"I'm fine, I swear. It's just the adrenaline wearing off." One tear leads to more and no matter how fast I am, I can't catch them all before they're streaming down my face.

"Actually, what I was going to say before you rudely interrupted me..." His eyebrow is cocked, his lips are twisted into an almost smile, and his tone is teasing. "is that I'm on the next flight out."

It takes my muddled brain a second to translate what he's saying. "You're what?"

"I'm coming to you. I'm heading to the airport now."

That's when I notice he's in a car. My heart leaps and I immediately sit up straighter. "You're coming here? You don't have to do that."

*But please come. Please, please come.*

Noel's smile is so self-satisfied and smug. "It's a good thing I didn't ask for your opinion. The flight's already booked."

More tears pour out of my defective eyes, but I feel lighter than I did moments ago. "What time are you landing?" I need to start a countdown clock—if I can hold on until Noel gets here, then everything will be okay.

"In a few hours. I'll send you the details." Noel pauses and something flashes across his face. Something that feels like a wet blanket over my nascent excitement.

"You haven't been on social media since yesterday, have you?"

I frown. "No, why?" I do recall seeing a lot of notifications on my phone last night, but I was a little preoccupied.

"Nothing. It's—don't worry. Don't look at anything until I get there."

Now I'm definitely checking all my notifications. "You can't tell me there's something there and then tell me not to look at it."

Noel scowls. "Just don't. Trust me. I'll be there soon and then we can go over everything together."

That doesn't sound ominous at all. "Noel, what the fuck?" My stomach twists at the increasingly angry expression on his face.

"I'm serious, Bell. Everything'll be okay. Better than okay! It's going to be great."

The more he says it, the less I believe it.

Noel lowers his phone to talk to his driver, then there's some fumbling as he gets out of the car. "Listen, I've got to go. Don't touch your phone until I call you again. I'm coming."

We disconnect the call and the first thing I do is check my notifications. I'm tagged in a video and a bunch of photos and what I see makes the blood drain from my face.

Jesus fucking Christ, how could I have been so stupid? There were dozens of people in that hotel lobby. The porn awards was happening a stone's throw away. Of course there were people there who recognized me and Noel.

It seems like the porn world didn't sleep a wink last night. My entire feed is full of the two of us. Our kiss on the curb has been turned into a GIF. The photo of Noel standing alone on the sidewalk is now a meme.

There's even a full-length article published in the early hours of this morning, detailing every single interaction we've ever had and ending in speculations about our relationship. What's real? What's fake? Have we been lying to our fans all these years? Is the whole rivalry nothing more than an elaborate publicity stunt?

The comments on social media are worse. Without the need to appear objective and professional, fans pour every thought and emotion into those comments in a stream of consciousness.

Noel and I are frauds, we're con artists, we're criminals. We're liars and cheaters and we should refund every cent we've made as camboys. There's even a conspiracy theory that we're agents of a foreign government sent to infiltrate American society. What the actual fuck?

I can't breathe. My heart is in my throat. I'm not physically dying, but good god, it feels like it. Snippets of my life flash before my eyes: hours locked in my bedroom with the crappy camera on my laptop; the first time I bought some decent equipment; my first collab; winning the Grabby's. Then Noel. The tug of a smile when he says something caustic about me. The way he pouts and fumes when I land a particularly good jab. Las Vegas. New York. Los Angeles.

Everything I've worked so hard for. The years spent building up my career brick by brick, one subscriber at a time. I could lose all of it because of a single moment of thoughtlessness.

Except, I can't. Not when Dad's lying unconscious in a hospital bed down the hall. Not when Twyla's set to go to college next fall. I'm supposed to take care of them, make sure they're okay. How can I do that if my fans decide they don't like me anymore?

I jump when my phone buzzes in my hand. It's Mom and I quickly wipe away the tears lingering in my eyes before answering the call.

"Hello, dear. Twyla and I are on our way back. We're going to pick up some breakfast along the way. Would you like anything?"

Breakfast. There's something about breakfast… what is it? *Enough coffee you'll be jittery for days.* Noel.

"Actually, Mom, you don't need to do that. It's already on its way." And if I know Noel, he'll order way more than we can eat.

"There is? From where?"

"Uh…" How do I explain who Noel is? Who he was, who he might become… why he's suddenly going to show up in a couple hours? "It's kind of a long story."

Mom says something to Twyla that the phone doesn't pick up, then she's back. "Okay, honey, if you're sure."

"I am. You can come straight here."

After we hang up, I close my eyes and lean against the cold concrete wall. I bang my head against it a couple times and welcome the pain radiating across my skull.

I should've expected this. It always happens. When things start going too well, life finds a way to bring me back down. When I think I've got it all figured out, life rears up to humble me again.

Who do I think I am to want a thriving career, a family who can take care of themselves, and a guy who loves me? One is fine. Maybe I could even get away with two. But all three? Don't be greedy, Bellamy.

Wait. I straighten. A guy who loves me? Love hasn't factored into our relationship at all and we've certainly never said the words out loud. But now that I think about it, it fits. I don't know what love feels like and I can't be sure that Noel loves me. But there's something there when we touch, when our eyes meet.

I push to my feet and wait for my head to stop spinning, for the pain flashing behind my eyes to fade.

Isn't love supposed to be some sweeping romance? A whirlwind that ends in a grand gesture? With Noel, it's been more of a slow and steady crawl. We've inched toward each other and chipped away at our respective defenses. That can be love, too, can't it? I can only hope.

# CHAPTER
# TWENTY-SEVEN

## NOEL

Exactly three hours and forty-six minutes after I hang up with Bellamy, I'm standing in the lobby of the hospital waiting for him to come fetch me. I'm not usually one for self-doubt, but I'm struck by it all of a sudden.

I've never been here before—where it feels like I have so much on the line. All the public backlash still pouring onto the internet. Showing up at his dad's hospital uninvited. I've always done whatever I wanted, taken whatever I wanted. But I don't know what to do right now, I'm not sure what I want.

True to his word, Sebastian spent all night with me like he was afraid I might do something rash if left on my own. He drafted a statement I barely glanced at and posted it on The Camboy Network's official accounts. It hasn't stemmed the attacks coming our way, but a small contingent of supporters have risen to our defense. Our next steps will have to be decided once Bellamy is brought up to speed. Except the last thing Bellamy needs right now is this kind of insipid distraction.

"Hey."

I spin around just in time for Bellamy to crash into me. Face pressed against my neck, arms wrapped tight around my body, he clings to me like he's drowning and I'm his last lifeline. I hug him back just as fiercely, absorbing all the exhaustion, frustration, and sadness coming off him in waves.

My momentary spell of doubt evaporates the instant Bellamy makes contact. Everything *is* going to be okay because I won't accept any other option. The thing about my being entitled and arrogant and pretentious is that I have the zeros in my bank account to back it up. Whatever happens, I'll throw so much money at it that it'll drown in all the green.

"You're here."

"I told you I was coming." If I sound cocky, it's because I am.

He pulls back and regards me with a dubious look that quickly succumbs to fatigue. "I know, I just…" His hands float up to bracket my face and his thumbs brush softly, reverently over my cheeks. "I thought I might've been dreaming."

I hit him with my smolder. "I am pretty dreamy."

He huffs a chuckle and leans his head on my shoulder with a sigh. "I went on social media."

So much for trying to spare him. "I told you not to."

"Did you really think I would listen?"

I had hoped. He shouldn't have had to read through all that vitriol by himself. "So you saw Sebastian's statement?"

"No, what statement?"

"I'll show it to you. He's got ideas for a counter-offensive but we wanted to get your input first."

Bellamy goes so still that for a moment it feels like he's fallen asleep in my arms. But then his chest expands with a deep inhale, and when he speaks, his weariness stains every word. "Okay. We might as well go upstairs then. My mom and sister have been asking about you all morning."

Bellamy weaves his fingers between mine as we turn toward the elevator, and my heart does a little flip-flop at the idea of holding hands with him in public. It's such a small thing, but I've never held hands with anyone like this before.

"Really?"

"Yeah, really," he laughs. "How else was I supposed to explain the mountain of food you ordered? We ended up giving half of it to the nurses." He doesn't sound nearly as grateful as he should.

"How am I supposed to know what you guys liked? I had to order a bit of everything."

"And enough coffee to power a space station."

I freeze mid-step and Bellamy turns to give me a quizzical look.

"You asked for extra coffee," I say, tugging my hand out of his and planting it on my hip.

He rubs my arms with a mollifying expression. "Aw, are you feeling pouty?"

"I don't pout."

"Mmhmm, no, of course you don't."

I take a step to close the distance between us. Electricity arcs even though he's dead tired and I'm not much better, even though we've got multiple fires we're trying to put out at the same time. This spark of ours, I don't think it'll ever die.

"Fuck you," I whisper against his mouth before catching his lips in a kiss.

He lets out a surprised whimper and melts into me. Our bags are forgotten on the floor. Maybe there's a supply closet nearby and we can pick up where we left off last night.

Bellamy eventually breaks the kiss with a murmured, "come on, we should go."

In the elevator, we drift into each other's arms again. He leans his forehead against mine and we rest there, breathing the same air and soaking in each other's presence. A peacefulness settles over us, calming the jittery unease I feel whenever I'm not with him. It's been less than twelve hours since I packed him into that taxicab, but even that is too long to be apart.

We're still holding hands when Bellamy leads me into his dad's hospital room, and it doesn't escape his mom or his sister's notice. His mom's eyes—Marla, if I remember correctly—lights up, while Twyla gives us a teenager-appropriate side-eye.

"Mom, Twyla, this is Noel."

"The breakfast guy," Twyla says. It's not a question.

Marla comes around the hospital bed and immediately pulls me into a full-bodied hug. "Thank you so much."

The unexpected affection is startling and it takes me a moment to hug her back. But when I catch Bellamy's eyes over Marla's shoulder, they're a little watery. Emotions have been running high around here. Some zealous hugging is warranted. "It was no problem."

Bellamy's dad stirs all of a sudden and I step back as everyone's attention turns to him.

"Dad? Can you hear me?" Twyla bends over the side of the bed.

He lets out a quiet moan and tries to reach for the oxygen mask over his face.

"No, Dad, you've got to keep that on." Bellamy pushes his hand down to the bed again.

"Bell?" Gene immediately breaks into a coughing fit and everyone holds their breaths until it dies down.

"Yeah, Dad, it's me."

"What're you doin' here?" Gene's voice, rough and slurred, is barely a whisper.

Bellamy scoffs exaggeratedly, more animated than I know he feels. "Where else would I be?"

"I'm fine." Which he promptly contradicts with another coughing fit.

The doctor arrives in the middle of it, joined by a nurse, and we all stand around awkwardly until Gene stops.

"Hi, I'm Doctor Coulter," the man in the white coat says. "I wanted to pop in and see how our patient is doing. How are you feeling, Gene? Breathing easier?"

Gene makes a non-committal sound that makes me think that breathing easily isn't a thing he's done in years. The nurse scoots around Bellamy to start fiddling with the beeping machine.

"Well, we're still waiting on some test results, but we suspect that you had a blood clot in the arteries around your lungs and that's what's caused all the fluid buildup. It's a good thing you came in because this condition can be fatal if not treated immediately." Dr. Coulter references the chart he's holding. "We've got you on blood thinners to help with the clots and diuretics to help drain the fluid. We'll keep you another day or two to make sure everything's clear before you go home."

"But what caused the blood clot in the first place?" Bellamy asks with a frown.

The doctor gives a shrug that's not at all confidence-boosting. "It could be a number of reasons and unfortunately, with Gene's condition as it is, this might become a more common occurrence."

"Are you saying it's just random?" Twyla's arms are aggressively crossed and her face is arranged in a scowl that even I'm impressed by. "It could happen whenever?"

"We'll adjust his medication and increase the dosage of blood thinners. Regular physical activity can also go a long way to prevent them."

Twyla's eye-roll is epic. "Yeah, right, good luck with that," she mutters.

Marla gives her arm a warning squeeze. "Thank you, Doctor. We appreciate you stopping by to give us an update."

Twyla flops herself into a sad-looking recliner when the doctor leaves. "You know Dad's never going to do any exercise."

"Hey." Gene's objection is barely more than a grunt.

"It doesn't have to be a three-mile run." Bellamy throws a glare at his sister. "Just walking around a bit counts too."

"I should've been better at getting you up on your feet every day." Marla shakes her head like she's disappointed in herself.

"Mom," Bellamy objects. "It's not your fault."

She casts him a sweet smile. "Thank you, dear. But this is important, I need to make it a priority."

"Mom—" He's cut off by his own yawn, his body waving the white flag of defeat.

Marla grabs her purse and pulls out a set of keys. "Why don't you go home and get some rest, dear? You've been here all night."

"I'm fine. I'm not tired. I can stay."

Marla swings the keys toward me instead. "Noel, can you take him home?"

There's no heat in the glare Bellamy shoots me, he's too exhausted for that. Besides, I rarely do what Bellamy tells me and I don't intend to start now.

"There are leftovers in the fridge if you guys get hungry," Marla says.

"But what if something happens while I'm gone?"

"We can handle it, dear."

"We handle it all the time when you're not around," Twyla mutters from the recliner, loud enough that it was clearly meant for Bellamy's ears.

The comment hits him like a physical blow and he deflates even further into himself. My anger flares, hot and immediate, and I bite my lip to hold back the retort on the tip of my tongue. Twyla's just a moody teenager, I remind myself. She's under a lot of stress with college applications and her father being ill. She has no clue how much Bellamy sacrifices for this family.

"Twyla," Marla chides.

"It's okay, Mom. She's right. You guys do handle it when I'm not around."

I grab Bellamy's arm and resist the urge to shake him. He can't possibly believe what Twyla's saying.

"Come on, let's go." I push Bellamy toward the door. We need to get out of here before I say something inappropriate. Besides, Twyla's the least of our worries. Bellamy and I have other problems to deal with. "Let's get you to bed."

**CHAPTER**
# TWENTY-EIGHT

## BELLAMY

The basement of the house I grew up in is exactly the same as it was while I was in high school. Futon in the corner. Plastic milk crates for a closet. A foldout table for a desk paired with a wobbly dining room chair. On the other end of the basement sits the washer and dryer, right next to the bathroom. The whole thing is only half finished.

Under normal circumstances, it might've been embarrassing to bring Noel down here, but I'm too tired to care. I told Mom I wasn't, but then I fell asleep on the car ride home, and getting down the stairs is a half-stumble, half-floating affair. By the time I flop face-first onto the futon, I'm basically unconscious.

Noel's hands are gentle as he removes my shoes and even more so as he manhandles me while taking my clothes off. I'm still wearing the suit from the awards show. The white carnation he pinned to the front of my jacket looks as wilted and crushed as I feel.

"Come on, into bed." Noel yanks the covers out from

under me and tucks me in. He starts to step away, but a sudden panic seizes me.

My hand shoots out from under the covers surprisingly fast and I grab his wrist. "Wait. Stay with me. Please."

Noel brings my hand to his lips and kisses the back of it. Then he strips down to his briefs and slides in next to me. I curl around his long, lithe body, hooking my leg over his hips to press us close. My eyes drift shut and I fill my lungs with the scent of him, losing myself in the cocoon Noel's made for us.

But sleep doesn't come.

I lay there with Twyla's parting comment playing on repeat in my mind. *We handle it all the time when you're not around.* It might not be fair, but it's accurate. I work hard and hustle, but I'm not here for the day-to-day. I don't have to watch Dad struggle with the stairs or listen to his coughing fits. I don't have to drive him to doctor appointments and pick up his medication from the pharmacy. In some ways, I've got it easy.

"Can't sleep?" Noel whispers into my hair.

"How could you tell?"

"Besides all the fidgeting?"

I groan and roll onto my back, throwing my arm over my eyes. They're so tired, they sting when I try to open them.

"What's going on in there?" Noel taps me on the forehead like he's trying to see whether it's hollow behind my skull.

I knock his hand away, but then slot our fingers together. "I don't know. Maybe I should move back here."

Noel pushes himself up onto an elbow and regards me skeptically. "Seriously?"

I move a shoulder in a semblance of a shrug. "They need the help. My career's probably over anyway. What's the point?"

Any hint of amusement dissolves from Noel's expression and his voice takes on an edge of steel. "Your career isn't over." He sounds so decisive. As if he can make it true simply by saying the words out loud.

I wish that was possible. Wouldn't it be great if Noel waved his magic credit card and all my troubles vanished into thin air? Wouldn't it be wonderful if I could stop juggling a million things at once and let it all smash into the floor? Sometimes the temptation is so potent I can practically taste it.

"Bell." Noel pokes me in the stomach when I don't respond and his scowl deepens when I can't work up the will to poke him back. He leans over me so his face is inches from mine. "Hey, dick face. Listen to me. You're not allowed to give up. Whatever's going on with your dad, whatever's happening with all that social media crap, we'll figure it out. Got it?"

I believe him. In some highly logical, completely unemotional part of my brain, I know he's right. But that doesn't make it any less exhausting and overwhelming and generally crappy. I don't want to suck it up and be strong and fix things anymore. I don't want to be the responsible one, the competent one, the one everyone else depends on.

I need someone to make it all go away.

Noel would do it if I asked. He wouldn't hesitate to whip out the plastic and start a running tab for Dad's medical care, for Twyla's college expenses, for this shabby house that could use a major renovation.

If only it was that easy. If only I could throw up my hands without getting eaten up by guilt. But I can't do that. We don't live in a fairy tale and I can't ask him to swoop in and save the day. I can only take comfort in this short stretch of time we have together.

I lift my head off the pillow and capture his lips with mine. After his initial surprise, he kisses me back, soft and gentle, and the urgency inside me roars for more. I surge up, tackling him onto his back. My lips find his jaw, the dip behind his ear, the column of his neck. I'm hungry for him, for the bliss I know I'll find in his arms.

"Bell," Noel says, confusion and laughter in his voice. "What are you doing?"

"What does it look like I'm doing?" I roll us again. Not to pin him under me, but to lay myself out for him. "Please, Noel." I arch up, urging him to take charge, looking for that big, domineering, aggressive personality I know he can be. I want him to hold me still, force me to surrender, and relinquish control.

A desperate sob escapes my throat. "Please, make me forget."

Noel holds himself above me, his gaze intent and searching. The instant he decides, his eyes darken danger- ously. With a growl, he digs his fingers into my flesh and descends upon me with his mouth. His tongue barrels its way past my lips and I moan at how right it feels to have him kiss me like this.

He doesn't need me to explain. He doesn't need justifi- cations or to be convinced. He never has. It doesn't matter what I ask for, Noel is always willing to give it to me, always willing to do whatever it takes.

He throws the covers off us and shucks his briefs off.

The musky smell of him hits my senses when he arranges his knees on either side of my head. His cock is already hard with pre-cum beading at the tip. I lick it, savoring the salty, bitter taste on my tongue.

*Thwack.* Noel's cock lands on my cheek and I gasp at the lewdness of it. *Thwack*—again, on the other side. My tongue is out as I try to chase his dick with my mouth. He feeds his balls to me instead. Heavy and full, they force my jaw wide. The warm, hard metal of his perineum piercing presses into my chin.

I bathe his balls, lavishing them, sucking on the skin of his scrotum. Noel pulls them out of my mouth and rubs them all over my face, leaving me wet with my own saliva, drowning in it.

He shifts farther up and sits right down on my face, burying my nose in his balls. My mouth is full of his taint and his piercing lands on my tongue.

"Suck it," Noel commands, rolling his hips and wiggling left and right. He settles himself more firmly on me, smothering me with his crotch.

I grab the tops of his thighs and hold him to me like I'm feasting on the most delicious meat. I lick, bite, mouth, working over his taint until it's swollen and pulsing on my tongue. I suck on his guiche, thrilling when he shudders above me.

"Fuck, Bell!"

My dick jerks at the sound of my name on his lips. It throbs in my underwear, desperate for friction, for release. But when I reach for myself, Noel grabs my wrists.

"No, no touching."

I whine into his crotch, sending another bout of shudders through him. He lifts himself off my face and lets me graduate to his cock. I moan in appreciation as he slides into me, all the way to the back of my throat and then farther down. I swallow around him, taking every inch he has, choking when he triggers my gag reflex. Noel only gives me enough time to suck in a single breath before he's coming in again, deep into me, cutting off my airway.

He fucks my face, my throat, making me gurgle with too much spit. I drown in him, in the smell of his musk, the taste of his pre-cum, the sweat dripping off him and landing in my eyes. My world is his cock stretching me wide, his balls slapping against my chin, my nose smooshed against his pelvic bone. He fucks every stray thought from my mind until there's nothing but Noel, Noel, Noel.

He comes with a roar, his cock lodged in the back of my throat. It swells and jerks on my tongue and his cum bypasses all my tastebuds, going straight down my esophagus. Lungs burning, heart racing, I'm on the verge of blacking out when Noel pulls out and collapses to my side. The sudden rush of oxygen sends my head spinning. My skin tingles, limbs tremble, dick a ticking time bomb between my legs.

Noel breathes heavily next to me, head on the same pillow. Each exhale sends a puff of warm air over my neck. He reaches down to carefully draw my briefs down my thighs, then takes my hand and brings it to my face. There's a filthy squelching sound when my palm lands on my cheek and drags through the saliva he painted me with.

"Touch yourself."

I'm afraid to. There so much blood in my erection it hurts.

"Jerk yourself."

Slowly, cautiously, my fingers wrap around my length and I suck in a hiss at the first drag of my palm over the ultra-sensitive organ.

"Harder. Faster."

I try, but the painful pleasure is too much and my nerve endings start firing chaotically all over my body. I cry out, releasing my dick at the random muscle spasms.

"Come on, Bell. You can do it. Make yourself come."

I try again, except this time, Noel covers my hand with his to make sure I don't back out. A yell rips from my throat at his tight grip, at his furiously fast pace. Fire, white hot, races along my length, straight down to my balls, then out to every corner of my being.

The orgasm rips through me, shredding everything in its path. Noel doesn't let up, stroking me again and again and stirring up surging waves of tortuous bliss. I'm torn apart. I'm destroyed. Noel reduces me to a sobbing mass of flesh and bones and I never want to be put back together.

# CHAPTER
# TWENTY-NINE

## NOEL

Watching Bellamy sleep is quickly becoming one of my favorite activities in the world. That fan of dark blonde lashes over his cheeks. The plump pout of his bottom lip. He makes these most adorable little sounds at the back of his throat right before he snuggles deeper into me.

A part of me wants to wrap him up and kidnap him, take him back to New York with me, and lock him in my apartment. I'd pamper him. Spa days with massages, facials, and mani-pedis. Deck him out in haute couture. Eat at Michelin-starred restaurants. I'd take him to Paris, Milan, Barcelona. We'd get a yacht and float around the Mediterranean. I'd make sure his family was taken care of, and we'd tell the porn world to fuck off because we don't need them.

Bellamy stirs and stretches, muscles lengthening, body arching and I can't resist running my hand down his side. He settles and turns to look at me, eyes still heavy with sleep.

"What time is it?"

"Mid-afternoon, I think."

"Shit." He runs a hand down his face. "We should get back to the hospital."

"How about a shower first?"

Bellamy peers at me from between his fingers. "Together?"

"Can't get enough of my cock?" I slide my hand across his hip and dip down to his inner thigh.

"Just trying to save water."

Tease. I catch his nipple between my teeth and when I bite, his dick twitches in my palm. My fingers massage it gently, encouraging it to swell in my hand.

"Come on." Bellamy slides out of bed and leads me into the small bathroom at the other end of the basement. The shower isn't big enough for two people, unfortunately, so we end up taking turns and not saving any water at all.

By the time I'm done and dressed, Bellamy's already upstairs in the living room, staring at an old ratty armchair that would look more at home in a landfill. The other furniture isn't much better. In fact, the whole house is kind of shabby—perfectly clean, don't get me wrong, but maintenance and upkeep can only go so far. The walls could use a fresh coat of paint and the carpet is threadbare. The only saving graces are the houseplants that dot each room.

"Hungry?" he asks. "Mom left tuna casserole in the fridge."

Ask me if I know what a tuna casserole is. "Sure."

The kitchen isn't much better than the living room. Decades of cooking have stained the cabinets yellow and battered the laminate countertops. The refrigerator's motor rumbles and ticks when it should be silent.

"You said Sebastian had a plan? About the… you know." Bellamy busies himself, taking a white ceramic dish out of the fridge and plating up the gooey, crunchy-looking beige stuff.

I take a seat at the tired kitchen table. "An idea for a plan. But he wanted your input first."

"I'm sure whatever he comes up with is fine." Bellamy sticks one plate into the microwave and when he hits start, the hum is so loud, we'd have to shout over it.

I watch him, leaning against the counter, arms crossed, gaze glued to the floor. He still looks tired, but more than that, he feels tired. The fatigue coming off him is thick and heavy and suffocating.

The microwave dings and he grabs a kitchen towel to take the plate out. "Careful. It's hot," he says when he sets the plate in front of me.

I stare at the mush. If I was judging it on presentation alone, I'd be on Uber Eats so fast. But the smells wafting from the plate make my mouth water. I poke at it suspiciously with a fork.

"It's not going to kill you, I promise. It's actually really good." Bellamy hits the microwave's start button so I can't even argue with him.

I suppose it can't hurt to try. I mean, those mushy cold fries in Los Angeles were surprisingly satisfying. Slowly, I take a small bite. It tastes exactly the way it smells. There's no nuance to the flavor, nothing delicate or complex. But the cheesy, savory taste hits the spot—a cozy homey spot that I didn't even know existed. I scoop up a larger bite.

"See? Good, right?" Bellamy smirks as he sits down across from me with his own plate.

I make a mental note to compliment Marla when I see

her next, but I'm not about to admit anything to Bellamy. His foot bumps into mine under the table and hooks around my ankle to trap it. I mimic the motion and our little foot sandwich fills me with as much warmth as Marla's tuna casserole. Our gazes meet and my breath hitches with a sudden overwhelming surge of love.

"I'm really glad you're here," he whispers.

Love wells up inside me, so much and so powerful I can't contain it. "I love you."

No panic or terror follow my words. Only a calm peacefulness that comes with knowing I'm exactly where I'm supposed to be. Emotions flicker across Bellamy's face as he processes, understands, and reacts. He regards me, slack-jawed. It doesn't matter what he says in response, or whether he even returns my feelings. I love him and I can't keep it hidden anymore.

Bellamy sucks in a gasping breath like he's resurfacing after a deep dive underwater. Then he says in a rush, "I love you too."

I didn't think I could get any happier, any more joyful, any more overflowing with love. But at Bellamy's words, I am, I do. I'm not aware of when it happened, but some of his sunshine has worked its way into me, lighting me up from the inside out. It grows and expands until I'm bursting with it.

I drop the fork, push my chair back, and stalk around the kitchen table. Bellamy pulls me into his lap so I'm straddling him, and I don't waste a moment before I shove my tongue down his throat. He moans around it, sucks on it like he's a starved man. His hands slip under my shirt and his fingers scour my back.

"Say it again," I murmur against his lip.

"I love you, you pompous, egotistical asshole."

I smile at the endearments. "I love you too, you self-righteous, arrogant prick."

We slam our mouths together and it's a while before we manage to get back to Marla's tuna casserole.

———

"So, Sebastian wants us to come clean?"

We're on our way to the car rental agency where I've got a car reserved. As far as we know, it'll be a couple days before Bellamy's dad can come home and then Bellamy will want to stick around to make sure he gets settled. I'm not about to leave Bellamy's side, so we figured we'd get our own car rather than share Marla's.

"Essentially." I pull up Sebastian's latest email that outlines his bullet-proof three-point plan. "We'll do an exclusive interview to 'tell our love story in our own words,' then a few publicity events together, then a sequel to our video."

Bellamy taps his fingers on the steering wheel. "He's sure it's going to work?"

Sebastian's an anxious mess most of the time, so he's never really sure about anything. But he's got an uncanny knack for business-y things like this. "He's rarely wrong."

Bellamy shrugs and sighs. "Okay, sure, I guess I'm cool with it."

Good thing we're not banking on his level of enthusiasm to win the public over. Good thing we're not banking on mine either, because I'm even less enthusiastic about it than he is. The fact that we have to do anything at all grinds me the wrong way, never mind all this kissyfaced glad-handing Sebastian's got planned for us. That's much more his brand—not mine.

"How are things looking now, anyway?" Bellamy asks. He sounds casual, but I can hear the thread of worry in his voice.

Neither of us have been on social media all day. Me, because I'll blow a gasket if I have to read any more of those comments. Bellamy, because I've confiscated his phone.

"Sebastian's ecstatic."

Bellamy shoots me a sideways glance. "Ecstatic?"

"According to him, the more chatter there is, the better. He wants people to be loud and opinionated about us so everyone else will want to see what the fuss is all about. Apparently, the numbers on the video are actually going up. He says it's all the hate-watchers."

Bellamy snorts. "Hate-watchers?" He signals and waits for the traffic to clear before turning into the car rental parking lot.

"You know, people watching it to see if they could tell we were, I don't know, whatever." Personally, I don't care why they're watching—by the time they hit play, we've already got their money.

Bellamy pulls into a parking spot and turns off the engine. Instead of getting out though, he reaches his hand toward me, palm up. I put mine in his, threading our fingers together.

"You know, a part of me is relieved." He regards our hands—my pale skin next to his tan—with quiet contemplation.

"Relieved?"

"That we don't have to hide anymore."

My heart leaps in my chest at what that means—for us, for our future. I've never been one to think too much about what I want my life to look like. It is what it is and I can usually buy anything that's missing. But I've never factored in love, and now I don't want a future without it. I want Bellamy in my life, every day, forever.

# CHAPTER
# THIRTY

## BELLAMY

For someone who's never been in a relationship before, Noel sure knows how to be a model son-in-law. My parents fucking love him. Twyla was a harder sell, but she's come around too. The constant trips to the frozen yogurt place certainly helped.

So do the fresh flowers he keeps buying for the kitchen. And the lunches and dinners that appear out of thin air, right when we're starting to feel hungry. It's good food too —none of that fancy shit in tiny portions that costs a fortune. I take credit for Noel's improved taste in cuisine.

He came with me to the medical devices store to pick up an oxygen machine for the house and helped me drive Dad home from the hospital. Since then, he's sat through endless games of baseball. Commendable, especially considering he was more interested in the tight pants the players wore than the games themselves.

I think I've fallen more in love with Noel in the past couple days than I did in all the months we've been secretly seeing each other. Who the hell would've guessed that bad boy, entitled asshole Noel Carrington had such a heart of gold? I did.

We end up staying in Cleveland for a little over a week. I wanted to stay longer and hide from the real world for a few more days, but Project Rehabilitate Noel and Bellamy's Public Image is already in motion and we're needed to keep it moving.

"It was so wonderful to meet you, Noel." Mom's got him in a bear hug so tight I wonder if she'll ever let go. "Make sure you come back to see us often, okay?"

"I will, Marla. Promise."

"And take care of Bell, too?" she says this part quietly, as if I won't be able to hear her from two feet away.

Noel nods, expression solemn like he's making some kind of vow. "I'll take care of him. You don't have to worry about that."

I can't help but roll my eyes. "Hello, I'm standing right here. I know how to take care of myself."

Mom pulls me into her arms. "Yes, I know, dear. But Noel's better at it than you are." She pats me on the cheek before stepping back from the BMW SUV that Noel rented.

We've already said goodbye to Dad and Twyla. Our bags are packed and stashed in the back of the car. There's nothing left to do but climb in and drive away. And yet…

"Mom," I start, but I don't know how to continue. I've visited them dozens of times since moving away from home, but this trip feels different. Maybe it's having Noel here or maybe it's the mess awaiting us when we get back to San Francisco. Either way, leaving feels more significant this time, like everything is about to change.

"I know, dear." She takes my hands in hers.

How does she know when I don't have the slightest clue?

"Don't worry about us," she says with that mom voice that always makes things feel more absolute. "We're going to be fine. And you're only a phone call away if we need you."

"I am. Whenever you need me."

"Noel's a good man. He's good for you." She gives me an indulgent smile. "Stop fighting him so much when he wants to help."

*Fighting is what we're good at.* It's on the tip of my tongue, but I doubt she knows about our rivalry and I'd rather she never finds out.

"You've worked so hard for so long, dear. I'm glad you don't have to do it alone anymore."

Some of the tightness in my chest unravels at her words, like they were the permission I needed to let go of the burdens I've carried around on my own. Noel's proven —to me, to all of us—that he's not afraid to get his hands dirty. He jumped right in and fit himself into my family like he's always been a part of it, until I couldn't remember how we ever functioned without him here.

What would life be like if I let him do that every day? If I let him use his money and his resources to make life just a little bit easier?

Mom kisses me on the cheek, then pushes me away. "Have a safe flight. Call me when you get home."

"Bye, Mom. I love you."

"I love you too, dear."

I climb into the car and shut the passenger-side door with a thud.

"Ready?" Noel asks.

I glance at him and reach for his hand. As our palms touch and fingers intertwine, the rest of the tension falls away. I still have all the same worries about Mom and Dad and Twyla. I have no idea how Sebastian's plan is going to play out or what implications it'll have for my career. But none of that feels as big and looming as it did even a couple days ago. It feels smaller, more contained, manageable. All because Noel is here to face them with me.

"Yeah, ready."

———

We turn heads when we walk through SFO. A quick glance at Noel tells me he's noticed it too. Anywhere else, I might chalk it up to people gawking at two very attractive men holding hands in public. But this is San Francisco.

I won't go so far as to say we planned for this, but we certainly prepared for it. Noel spent a good fifteen minutes in the plane's lavatory fixing his hair so it has the perfect amount of muss.

Sure enough, photos start popping up on social media the minute we get into our rideshare. Noel shows me his phone with a smirk. I have to say, we look really fucking hot. Noel's in all black, with shades on even before we're outside. I'm in shorts and a rainbow t-shirt, with flip-flops on my feet. We are the epitome of dark and light, grumpy and sunshine, bad boy and golden boy.

A message from Sebastian pops up on the screen while I'm holding Noel's phone.

SEBASTIAN

Good job on the walk of shame.

Noel snorts and takes his phone back from me.

NOEL

You mean walk of fame.

In fact, we've been feeding social media tasty little morsels every day for the past week, getting them nice and hungry for the exclusive interview we've got lined up with *Adult Entertainment Weekly* later today. It was Sebastian's idea, of course. If fans were going to dissect every aspect of our relationship, then let's give them something to work with—something that suits *our* needs, not anyone else's.

The car takes us back to my apartment and Santino's standing in the middle of the kitchen when we walk in. In his hands are a knife and half a bagel and he's wearing nothing but a towel.

"Holy shit!" He drops the knife and the bagel when he sees us. Or rather, sees Noel. "You're him."

Noel pops his sunglasses on top of his head and shoots me an amused look. "Uh, yes?"

Santino stands there, jaw on the floor. If I didn't know better, I'd think he's fanboying over Noel.

I suppress a snicker and introduce them. "Santino, this is Noel. Noel, Santino."

That seems to snap Santino out of whatever starstruck trance he's fallen into.

"Hey, oh my god, hi. Yeah, dude, it's really cool to meet you."

Noel regards him warily. "Nice to meet you too."

Santino leans forward, as if he might go in for a hug, which is my cue to intervene. "Okay, well, we're just here to pick up a few things, then we're headed out again." I grab Noel's arm and drag him away.

"What was that?" Noel asks when we're safely ensconced in my room.

"I don't know. He's usually pretty chill. Maybe you've short-circuited his brain."

Noel fucking preens. "I've been known to do that."

"Fuck you." I laugh. Big changes might be on the horizon, but at least I can take comfort in the handful of things that will always stay the same.

I drop my big duffle on the bed, pull out the dirty clothes and replace them with clean ones. My suit from the awards show is wrinkled almost beyond hope, so it goes into the same pile as all the other laundry. I'm flipping through my closet when Noel interrupts.

"What are you doing?"

"Finding something to wear for the interview." I pull out a sports jacket.

"You don't have to do that." He takes the jacket from me and holds it up with an appraising eye. "Not bad. But unnecessary. I've arranged for a stylist to meet us at the hotel." He hangs the jacket back up.

"You're joking, right?" Except I can tell from his expression that he's absolutely not.

"No, why would I joke about something like that?" He actually looks a little offended, which if we were still in Cleveland, I might've found endearing. But we're back in the real world now and he can't go around buying stuff for me all the time.

I grab the jacket from the closet again. "I don't need a stylist. I have my own clothes and I can dress myself."

He's standing between me and the garment bag laid out on the bed, and despite the pointed look I cast him, he doesn't budge. In that moment, we're our old selves again

—facing off, both of us determine to win, neither willing to back down. The air crackles with electricity and it trips across my skin in tingles.

"Noel."

"Bell."

"Move."

His jaw ticks and I can hear the calculations he's running in his mind—how pissed will I be if he snatches the jacket from me and shoves it back into the closet? The answer is very goddamn pissed.

After a few long beats Noel finally steps aside. But instead of the rush of satisfaction I normally get, guilt tickles the back of my mind. Noel's just trying to *take care* of me, like he promised Mom he would. I drop the jacket on top of the garment bag with a sigh, then turn to him, slipping a hand onto his waist.

"I'll take a look at what the stylist brings and if there's anything I like…" I shrug and Noel's jaw relaxes.

"Fine."

"I love you."

Noel rolls his eyes. "I love you too."

# CHAPTER
# THIRTY-ONE

## NOEL

The interview with *Adult Entertainment Weekly* is in a restaurant on the Embarcadero, with views of the Bay Bridge. The clear blue sky extends out as far as the eye can see and the sun reflects off the calm, rippling waters of the San Francisco Bay. Bellamy and I arrive before the reporter and are shown to a table by the window.

He's wearing his own sports jacket, much to my chagrin. To his credit though, he did look through the options brought by the stylist and even I have to admit that his own jacket looked best on him. I'll have to give more specific instructions the next time I bring a stylist in. We wouldn't want Bellamy dressing too much like me.

"Nervous?" I ask once we take our seats.

Bellamy fiddles with the utensils, lining them up just right, then shoots me a withering look. "No. Why would I be nervous? I've done interviews like this hundreds of times."

"Then why do you keep fidgeting?"

He stills, then slowly lays his hands flat on his thighs. "I'm not fidgeting."

I arch an eyebrow at him.

"Fuck you."

Yeah, that's what I thought. The energy coming off Bellamy has enough wattage to power the lights. "Don't worry. They'll be softball questions. Their job is to make us look good."

Bellamy takes a deep breath and lets it out in a low, steady sigh. "Right."

A petite woman in fashionable boyfriend jeans and a sharp blazer approaches our table. "Noel Carrington. Bellamy Blais." She stops with one hand on her hip as she looks between us like she can't believe what she's seeing. "When my editor told me about this interview, I thought it was a practical joke. But here you both are."

I stand to shake her hand. "You must be Freya Lawson."

"That, I am."

When I step aside to let Bellamy greet her, he's got his practiced smile on, eyes twinkling, posture open and welcoming. There isn't a trace of the nervousness plaguing him a moment ago. Only poise and grace and charm—a consummate professional.

"Well," Freya says after we've taken our seats and a waiter has come around with our drinks. "I have to admit, I feel like I'm waiting for a punchline."

Bellamy laughs, eyes crinkling at the edges. He glances toward me and our gazes catch. There's sunlight streaming in through the window—because of course there is—and the blues of his irises put the view of the water behind him to shame.

"Tell me about it," he says, not taking his eyes off me. "I still can't quite believe it myself."

A beat passes in silence as I lose myself in Bellamy's eyes. We're visiting a beach soon, I've decided. I want to compare his eyes to the blue of the water. I need to see if the scent of the real sun and ocean breeze lives up to Bellamy's version.

"I stand corrected," Freya says softly as she studies us. "I suppose you could be acting, but I don't think either of you are that good."

I drag my gaze away from Bellamy and shoot her a scowl. We might not be winning any Oscars, but we were good enough to fool everyone with our video.

Bellamy chuckles and grins self-deprecatingly. "No, we're not that good." He rests our clasped hands on the table. "And no, we're not acting."

"All right, then." Freya pulls out a hand-held recorder and sets it on the table between us. "Let's tell the world your story."

———

Forty minutes later, the interview is done and dusted, and Bellamy and I stroll back to our hotel, hand-in-hand.

"I can't believe you told her about the blowjob you gave me backstage at the Grabby's." Bellamy laughs.

I shrug. "She asked for juicy stories."

"They're never going to invite us to present again."

"If they're smart, they'll ask us to present every fucking year." I bump him with my shoulder. "And what the hell with the dick pics? I never sent you any dick pics."

Bellamy throws his head back. The wind tousles his

hair and sunlight makes the golden strands glow. "You sent me pictures of that dick piercing you want to get!"

"That's not my dick!"

"I never said it was," he insists.

"Fuck you."

"So when are you going to get it done?" He casts me a mischievous grin.

"The piercing?" I looked into it a while ago, but never seriously considered getting it done. With the way Bellamy's looking at me now though… "It would mean no fucking for a couple weeks."

"Maybe not for you." Bellamy lets go of my hand so he can grope my ass. "But I can do all the fucking I want."

A shudder runs through me at the prospect. A piece of metal through my cock, solid and heavy. The weight of it as Bellamy drives into me, the way it would make my cock swing. How it would feel when he rubs it, flicks it with his tongue.

Bellamy crowds me up against a building, hands on my waist, pulling us close to rub our growing erections together. "You're thinking about it, aren't you?"

All I can do is grunt.

"Are you thinking about my hands on you?" He leans forward to whisper in my ear while innocent bystanders walk past us. "I'll touch you everywhere, lick you everywhere except your cock. It'll be hard and leaking, but you couldn't do anything about it."

I clamp my hands on his shoulders and sway a little, lightheaded from all the blood rushing to my groin. My dick pulses and throbs, the tip extra sensitive like it's already wearing a piercing.

"Maybe we should look up body piercers. I'm sure

there are reputable ones who can squeeze in last-minute clients."

"Fuck, Bell."

"Is that a yes?" He smiles against the shell of my ear.

"That's a 'we need to get the fuck back to our room because I'm going to wreck your ass.'"

He chuckles, the sound winding through me, warm and full of all the things I love about him. When he slips his hand into mine, we practically sprint back to the hotel. The second he unlocks the door to our suite, I'm on him, pushing him up against the wall.

"Remember the first time you did this to me?" Bellamy gasps out between kisses.

"Vegas," I growl.

"God, you hated me so much back then."

"I'm going to hate you now if you don't shut up and get naked."

Bellamy's laughter rings out loud and clear as we strip. I'll never get tired of that sound, how bright and ringing it is, how it makes my heart flip over in my chest. I want to listen to that laugh every day for the rest of my life.

"You want this ass?" Bellamy inches toward the bedroom. "Come and get it."

I tackle him onto the bed, both of us naked and hard, fighting each other for control. We grapple and roll, skin sliding against skin. Bellamy gets me on my back, then slithers out of my arms, kissing and licking every inch of my body until he's got my cock in his hand and his lips poised an inch away.

"Where would it go?" His breath is hot on my already heated flesh, sending a shiver up my spine. "Right here?" He rubs his thumb back and forth on the underside of the head, in that super-sensitive spot just below the glans.

"And it would come out here." He digs his tongue into my slit and a pulse of pre-cum oozes into his mouth. My hips come up off the mattress, chasing the wet heat of his mouth, the tight constraint of his throat.

"I wonder how it would feel in my ass." Bellamy laves his tongue up and down my cock. "Do you think I'd feel it running over my prostate?"

"Fuck, Bell." That question had never once crossed my mind, but now I need to know the answer like it's the key to eternal happiness.

Bellamy wraps his lips around me and sucks me down. He hums when I thread my fingers through his hair and tug.

"How would blowjobs work?" He muses when he comes up for air. He's got tears in his eyes, his chin is wet with spit, and I can practically see the silver ring resting between his parted lips.

Fuck it. Enough of this teasing. I'm going to drive Bellamy into the mattress and then we'll look up body piercers.

"Come here." I haul him up to me and flip him onto his back with my hips wedged between his legs. I'm poised to shove myself into his body when I pause.

There's something in his eyes that steals my breath away. So much tenderness. All that affection. I kiss him, soft and gentle, pouring every ounce of love I feel into it. He kisses me back, his love overwhelming me in return.

Bellamy breaks off the kiss. "Lube," he whispers in a pleading voice.

I reach under a pillow and pull out the bottle.

"Seriously?" He chuckles in disbelief. "You hid lube under the pillow?"

"Of course I did. You should know me better by now."

I take my time prepping him, cataloging every expression that floats across his face, imprinting each into my memory. When I finally slide into him, I have to bite his shoulder to keep myself from sobbing. It feels so good—almost too good—to have him in my arms, his limbs tangled up with mine. To be inside his hot, tight channel, feeling him squeeze me as he takes me to the root.

It feels right, like this is the place I was always meant to be. Like everything in my life—in our lives—have merely been stepping stones bringing us to this moment. It feels like home, my sanctuary, my refuge, where I belong.

"Move in with me."

"What?"

Ignoring the moisture building on my lashes, I lift my eyes to look Bellamy in the eyes. I'm still buried inside him; his legs are still locked around my waist. "Move in with me. In New York. My apartment is big enough for both of us. Or we can find another place if you want."

Bellamy blinks like he can't quite process what I'm saying. "You're asking me this now?" He squirms, making us both gasp when he clamps down on my cock.

I lift a shoulder and somehow manage a nonchalant smirk. "I've got to press my advantage." I cant my hips, pushing deeper into him.

"Fuck, you're an asshole."

"I've never claimed to be anything else."

"Goddamn, I hate you sometimes."

I pull halfway out and punch my hips forward. "Is that a yes?"

"Fuck you."

"Actually, I think *I'm* fucking *you*." I give him another short, hard thrust. "So? What's your answer?"

"Yes, goddamn it. You motherfucking douchebag. Yes, I'll move in with you. Christ, can you fuck me now?"

I smile, not caring how goofy it looks. "With pleasure."

Except I don't. Fuck him, that is. He's turned me into a pathetic romantic sap, so he'll have to live with the consequences.

I make love to Bellamy. Slow and sweet, speeding up to drive us both crazy, backing off when either of us gets too close. We kiss, with lips and teeth and tongue, savoring the taste of each other.

"Noel, please." Bellamy eventually begs and the wretched need in his voice flips the switch in me.

I plunge into him, sure and steady, unrelenting as we both race toward the cliff, knowing that we'll always be there to catch each other.

# CHAPTER
# THIRTY-TWO

## BELLAMY

It turns out, we both have very opinionated fans. The *Adult Entertainment Weekly* article went live early on a Friday morning and our phones didn't stop dinging with notifications until well into the next week.

Some people thought we were bullshit, a less-than-unbelievable fairy tale, made up to cover our asses. Others thought we were the greatest love story since Romeo & Juliet. Whatever they thought, they shouted it all over social media at anyone who would listen to them—and even some who wouldn't.

There's always been fan fiction about us floating around the internet. I've never really paid much attention to them, but they've since exploded in popularity. The authors should end up with a book deal out of this— Sebastian, at least, has been chatting with a few about collaboration opportunities.

On balance, we've had more fans on our side than against. Downloads of our video skyrocketed to the point where Sebastian had to buy extra bandwidth for The Camboy Network website. And the comments are *rife*.

*See that right there? You can tell they have feelings for each other already.*

*Look at the way they're fucking, so much love!*

*No way. They definitely still hate each other. You can't fake that level of animosity.*

Noel's page has more than doubled its subscribers. Mine's inching closer to triple. The windfall means I've set aside a huge chunk of cash for Twyla's tuition fund. I've also started broaching the idea of hiring a nurse to stop by the house every day—Mom and Dad don't love it, but I might be able to convince them once Twyla's college plans become reality.

My phone buzzes with a notification that our rideshare is downstairs waiting for us. "Noel!"

"Yeah, one second!"

I don't know what's taking him so long since we'll both be stripping down to thongs and jockstraps soon. Monte's Manties got in touch with us a few hours after the news broke to book us for their float in New York's Pride Parade. The marketing person I spoke with on the phone couldn't stop gushing about the pivotal role they played in our grand romance.

They're not the only ones who've reached out. An LGBTQ community center invited us to be bachelors at their annual charity auction. They auctioned us off together—two camboys for the price of one. We made a point of putting on a live show for their guests. It was for a good cause, after all.

The dildo company The Camboy Network works with asked to revise their contract to include my dick in their product line-up. They're going to offer a special Noel and Bellamy dildo package as their Valentine's Day special next year.

"Noel!" I yell again. "We're going to be late!"

"I'm here. I'm here. Fuck, relax." He's wearing a pair of running shorts and a loose tank top—both of which will be stuffed into our bags the minute we get to the float. His hair is impeccably styled and he's got on a full face of makeup.

"You know they're giving us water guns, right?"

Noel gives me a dead-eyed stare. "If you shoot me with water…"

I crowd into his space, chin lifting in a challenge. "You'll what?"

He growls but when my hands settle on his hips, he can't help but melt into me. "I don't know," he grouses, "but you'll regret it."

"Uh huh, I'm sure." I kiss him, a light press at first, since I'm a considerate boyfriend and I don't want to smudge his lipstick.

But then I slide my hands past the waistband of his shorts and palm the round globes of his ass, left naked by his Manties thong. Noel lets out a groan and deepens the kiss, pushing his tongue into my mouth for me to suck on. My cock twitches against the fabric of my already too-tight jockstrap, and I grind myself against Noel to relieve the pressure.

"I thought we needed to go," Noel murmurs against my mouth.

I let out an irritated sound and reluctantly push him away. "You did that on purpose."

His still perfectly painted lips curl into a smirk. "I don't know what you're talking about."

"Come on, dick face." I grab my bag and we hurry down from Noel's penthouse apartment before the driver gives up on us and leaves.

Although I haven't officially moved in with him yet—the lease I share with Santino isn't up for another couple months and I don't want to leave him hanging—Noel and I haven't spent a single night apart since leaving Cleveland. If we're not in his apartment in New York, then we're in a hotel suite in San Francisco. He even followed me down to New Orleans for a photo shoot, because he "can't sleep without me next to him." I haven't stopped teasing him about that, but I was glad to have him there. I can't sleep without him next to me either.

With all the road closures, it takes us longer than expected to get to the parade's staging area. By the time we find the Monte's Manties float, we're the last ones to arrive.

"Oh, thank god!" The woman wearing a Manties t-shirt shoves water guns into our hands. "We weren't sure you guys would make it!" She points to the back of the float. "You can climb up that way. There's extra water to refill the guns when you run out. And remember, we want love and hate—shoot water at each other, wrestle, kiss, the whole thing."

Noel holds his plastic water gun away from him with two fingers, like it's a rotting fish.

Jesus, he's such a snob. "Come on, it's not that bad," I say, dragging him toward the float.

Once we've stripped down to our underwear and take our places in the middle of the float, it finally sinks in how wild this is. Around us are a handful of dancers, also wearing Monte's Manties, but we're up on a raised platform by ourselves, on display for the whole world to see.

I'm not exaggerating. The parade is being broadcast on cable, meaning my parents could turn on their TV and see me and Noel with our asses hanging out, shooting water at each other, and making out in front of millions. Being famous in porn is a pretty big deal, but it's nothing compared to this.

I'd be lying if I said I wasn't a little nervous. It's surreal, too good to be true, and I keep waiting for the other shoe to drop, for life to rear its ugly head and rip it all away.

"Hey, the face is off limits." Noel points a finger at me, his expression stony.

I aim my gun at his feet and send out a long spray of water.

Noel jumps back with a shriek. "What the hell?"

"I'm just testing it. Making sure it works."

"It fucking works!" Noel stares daggers at me. "Asshole," he mutters and my heart warms at the endearment.

"You love me!"

His scowl grows deeper for a second before softening with tenderness. "Fucker."

It's staggering how much I love this man, his entitled arrogance, his sulking grumpiness, his egotistical attitude. I love him so much I can't help but tease.

"Shit, I think I broke it," I say, fiddling with the firing mechanism on the toy.

"That's what you get for disrespecting me." Noel steps in to peer at my gun, like he's trying to help me with it.

When he's nice and close, I send a stream of water directly into his chest. The water splashes up onto his face and Noel freezes with a look of murder in his eyes.

"You are going to pay for that," he utters, voice dripping with venom. If this was anyone else, I might actually be scared. But Noel would never do anything to hurt me.

A giggle bubbles up in my chest. "Oh yeah? Who's going to make me?"

Noel lifts his water gun and the instant he takes aim, the floor beneath our feet jerks with the float's movement. He's thrown off balance but the railing around us keeps him from tumbling head-first onto the asphalt. My giggle bursts into belly-deep guffaws, which only makes Noel's expression darken even more.

"Aw, poor baby. Do you need me to teach you how to use the toy?"

"Motherfucker. I don't need a fucking toy."

With two strides, he's suddenly in my face. I raise my hand and it makes contact with his chest, but I know better than to believe that that will stop him. Noel doesn't swipe it aside though. We stand nose-to-nose, staring into each other's eyes.

The float inches forward. Music blares from the speakers around us. We turn a corner onto the main parade route and the roar of the crowd is deafening.

His heart races against the palm of my hand and the rise and fall of his chest matches my every breath. This is real—me and him—it's in the warm solid muscles under my fingertips, it's in the way he looks at me like I'm the only person in the universe.

In all my wildest fantasies, I never would've conjured up someone like Noel. Someone who keeps me on my toes and holds me tight at night, who insults me in one breath and moves heaven and earth to help me the next. He's everything I never knew I wanted, and there's not a single thing I would change.

A smirk grows on my lips and an identical one appears on Noel's. Time to put on a show.

We crash into each other with mouths and hands and legs. We grope and grasp and bite, tearing at one another with an urgency that makes my head spin. In the distance, crowds scream and chant our names, but here in this bubble, it's just the two of us.

When Noel finally steps back, I cling to the railing, lightheaded and unsteady on my feet. I'm still trying to find my bearings when Noel swings his water gun up and fires. A shriek escapes my throat as a steam of cold water hits me on the stomach.

Noel cackles in evil delight before turning to the spectators and showering them in water too. We dance. We spray water everywhere. We kiss and touch and rub up against each other. By the time the parade ends, my whole body is pruney, my lips are bruised and tender from all our kissing, and my cock has tried to escape the confines of my jockstrap at least a dozen times.

Sebastian, Christian, and Noel's two other friends, Rhys and Hayden, meet us as we hop off the float.

"Oh my god, you guys, you were amazing up there!" Sebastian runs forward and pulls first me, then Noel into a hug. "Like, so freaking hot!"

"You guys made the top ten floats of the parade!" Rhys says, holding up his phone for us to see the article that was published just minutes ago.

"Hell yeah, we better be." Noel preens, ego on full display.

"I think my eardrums burst when your float went by." Hayden laughs and massages his ear. "There was so much screaming."

Christian pats me on the shoulder. "Hey, good job."

"So! Party continues this way!" Rhys waves his hands in the air and starts shooing us down the street.

The Bronzed Rail is the club where Rhys dances a couple nights a week and where Monte's Manties is hosting a Pride party straight into the night. It's really only a few blocks from where we are, but it takes us a good forty-five minutes to get there. Every few steps, we're stopped by fans who want autographs and pictures—of me, of Noel, of us together, of us kissing. We're more than happy to oblige. These fans loved us when we were enemies and they love us now that we're together. And with every picture they post on social media, our profile grows that little bit more.

"Are you guys going to do another video?" a fan asks.

I've lost count how many times we've been asked this question and the truth is, Sebastian's already working on pre-production. But those plans are still under wraps at the moment.

"Yes! OMG, you have to!"

"Please! You guys are so good together!"

"I love you guys! You're the best!"

When we eventually make it to The Bronzed Rail, Noel takes my hand and weaves his way through the crowd. We slip past a bouncer and duck behind a rack of clothing backstage.

"Fucking finally," Noel murmurs as he grabs me and pushes me up against the wall.

His mouth slants over mine and I moan as our tongues meet. It doesn't matter that we've been kissing all day, I'll never get tired of Noel's lips, his tongue, his mouth. We're plastered from chest to knee, with nothing between us but the wet scraps of fabric barely covering our dicks. And yet it doesn't feel close enough. It won't ever be close enough. With Noel, I'll always want more.

"I fucking love you, Bell," he pants as we catch our breaths.

I wrap my arms tight around him, hike my knee up around his hip, and bury my face into the crook of his neck, closing my eyes as our hearts beat as one.

"I fucking love you, too, Noel."

# EPILOGUE

## BELLAMY

I shoehorn my way through the door, balancing a box in my arms while navigating around a maze of crap scattered throughout the apartment. "Babe?"

"In here!"

Dropping my box on the floor, I poke my head into the kitchen where Noel's scowling at an espresso machine wearing nothing but a pair of navy-blue bikini briefs. He looks so disgruntled I have to bite the inside of my cheek to keep from laughing out loud.

"What are you doing?" I saunter up behind him, hooking my chin over his shoulder while slipping my arms around his waist. He's warm where I press myself against him and I grind my growing erection into his ass.

"What does it look like I'm doing?" he grumbles, fiddling with the switches and nobs on the machine. "Stop distracting me."

"Hmm." I've absolutely no intention of stopping. In fact, distraction is exactly what I'm aiming for as my hand slides down his stomach to his cock, so hard it's threatening to pop out of his very tight briefs.

Noel lets out a low lusty sound and shudders in my arms.

"The espresso machine can wait. We need to christen the apartment." I tweak his pierced nipple, pleased with myself when Noel responds exactly as I wanted. He jolts, sucks in a hissing breath, and drops his head back on my shoulder—espresso machine forgotten. Over the past several months, I've learned exactly how to manipulate his piercings and I'm not above putting my new-found knowledge to good use.

I hook my thumb in his waistband and when I start dragging them down, Noel catches my wrist in his hand.

"Sensitive?"

He grunts in agreement. Poor thing. He's been walking around with a perma-chubby for the past three weeks and it doesn't look like it's going to change any time soon.

"Wait, hold on."

I pause at Sebastian's instructions.

"Babe, can you fix the light, please?" Behind him, Christian shifts a tripod to the left until Sebastian gives him a thumbs up. "Bellamy, let's do that again."

"Fucking hell," Noel mutters, shooting Sebastian a death glare. But he doesn't object when I pull his underwear back in place and drag the fabric over his hard, pulsing cock again.

I get it all the way down this time and his dick springs out, thick and heavy with an extra weight on the end—a weight that's been my new obsession. It's also why we've waited this long before shooting our follow-up video. Noel needed a couple extra weeks to heal from his dick piercing.

"Goddamn," I murmur with genuine reverence in my voice. I'm never going to tire of seeing the smooth, hard metal sticking out of Noel's flesh, the unexpected warmth of it, the way he jerks when I touch it. He says it feels like the piercing is connected to his prostate, that when I play with it, it's like I'm toying with that spot deep inside him.

The silver metal gleams under the lights and we all watch as a drop of pre-cum escapes Noel's slit. It trails down the underside of his cock and catches on the ring. My grip tightens around his dick, sliding from base to tip, and more pre-cum oozes out of him.

It's a waste really, watching all that juicy goodness spill out and not catching it on my tongue. Noel's pre-cum is a freaking delicacy and I make a point of getting my dose of it on a daily basis.

"Cut!" Sebastian calls out. "That's great. Let's move to the living room next."

I swipe my finger through the clear, sticky fluid and bring it to my lips. I think I'm more addicted to Noel now than I've ever been before. Every taste of him only deepens and fuels my need.

Living with Noel for the past couple months feels like home in a way I haven't experienced in a long time. I remember thinking his apartment was cold and imper-sonal at first, but now I can't imagine us living anywhere else. My clothes are in the closet, my toothbrush in the bathroom, and my laptop has its own spot on the coffee table. Sometimes I catch Noel gazing at me from across the room and my heart fills with so much love for him it aches.

"You guys ready?"

I reluctantly pull away from Noel, but when I turn to Sebastian, he's frowning at his phone. "Is everything okay?"

"Um, I don't know." His thumbs tap away for a moment before he looks up with a concerned expression. "It's Rhys. Something about his dad's birthday party."

"Oh. Shit." Noel cringes, so it must be bad.

"What's wrong?" I ask.

"Rhys's family is… well, they're not outright homo-phobic, but they're definitely homo-not-approving." Sebastian gives himself a shake. "Don't worry about it. I'll talk to him later." He nods toward the living room. "We're all set up."

Sebastian has Noel lie down on the couch in the middle of the room, surrounded by empty cardboard boxes. He's got a pillow behind his head and one foot planted on the floor.

I'm on the other end of the couch and when Sebastian calls "action," I work my way up Noel's body with my mouth. Toes, the arch of his foot, the back of his knee, the inner thigh, the crease of his hip. He's hard and the tight briefs do nothing to hide his erection—or the ring I put through it.

Okay, *I* didn't pierce his cock. But I was there when a professional did it. I couldn't tear my eyes away from the sight of Noel's dick being handled by a pair of hands wrapped in black latex. The needle pressed right up against the vulnerable flesh, and the terrifying give when it finally slid through. I was hard the entire time, leaking so much pre-cum I was afraid it would soak through my pants.

I like to think of it as *my* piercing, even though it's on

Noel's cock. I found the guy at the tattoo parlor to do the piercing. I picked out the jewelry. I decided it would be a frenum rather than a prince albert. It's mine. And I get to do whatever I want with it.

Like play. A shiver runs through me when my lips make contact with the hard steel ring, so unyielding against Noel's already hard cock. Above me, he groans and his hips come off the couch.

I push him down and lay myself across his legs to keep him from moving again. His cock lies on his stomach, and the silver metal sits right below his glans, on the underside where he's super sensitive. We haven't tried it yet, but the ring is big enough that we can twist it up over his cock and hook it behind the ridge of the head. I can't wait for Noel to fuck me like that.

Sneaking my tongue out, I wiggle it under the ring.

"Fuck, Bell."

Then I lift it up and let it drop, hard and heavy on Noel's cock.

"Oh god. Fuck." Noel stabs his fingers in my hair and tries to get my mouth around him.

I rub my face all over his dick instead, and my stubble scrapes against the vulnerable, delicate skin.

"Goddamn it, motherfucker!" His hand pushes me away. But his hips cant forward like he wants more.

"Do that again," Sebastian whispers to me from behind the camera.

Gladly. I slow it down this time and pre-cum gushes from Noel's cock.

"Jesus-fucking-Christ. I hate you. All of you. Especially you." He takes his dick with his free hand and shoves it between my parted lips.

I barely have a second to suck in a lungful of air before I'm stuffed full. My eyes drift shut and I relax as he stretches my jaw and fucks my mouth like he doesn't care if I pass out. When he eventually relents, I lay my head on his thigh to catch my breath. Noel's fingers are tender and gentle in my hair, brushing it back from my forehead.

"You're so fucking gorgeous," he says, voice full of wonder and awe.

I tilt my head up to look at him, caught in the love that's so evident in his eyes. He's gorgeous too. All dark and stormy, turbulent and explosive. Yet, he's my anchor in the chaos of life. He's my rock, sure and solid and safe.

I smile, heart so full that it sometimes feels like I'm going to burst open. Then I twist my lips. "Eh, you're all right, I guess."

Noel's eyebrows slam together, his gaze sharpens, and his jaw ticks in annoyance. "Asshole. Take it back."

I split into a shit-eating grin. Here we go. "Make me."

"Uh, guys?"

Noel levers up from the couch, grabbing me by the shoulders, and tries to flip me under him, but I fight back, wriggling for escape. We land in an *oomph* on the floor, with me on the bottom and the air knocked out of my lungs. "Fucker."

Noel's not done with me though. He sinks his teeth into my chest muscle, hard enough it feels like he might break skin.

"Motherfucker!" I bring my knee up between Noel's legs, wedging my thigh high and hard against his balls.

He squeaks, rearing back, and I roll us to pin him to the floor.

"Guys! Jesus Christ. You're both impossible."

I grab Noel by the chin, turn his head to the side and lick him with the flat of my tongue, from his jaw straight up to his temple.

"God-fucking-damn it!"

I laugh. I can't help it. I'm just so ridiculously happy that it comes bubbling out of me. How is it possible to love someone so much, so thoroughly, that every day feels like a dream come true?

I love it when we're playing around like this. I love it when we're sweet and affectionate with each other too. I can't imagine my life without him, whether he's grumpy and abrasive or overbearingly protective. He's everything I never knew I wanted. He's all I'll ever need.

## BONUS SCENE

Noel's knee is bouncing up and down so hard that I can feel it vibrating the seat of my chair. It's a wonder that the whole table isn't shaking.

I slap my hand on his thigh. "Smile, babe," I say through the grin plastered on my own face.

There are cameras all over the damn place, including one zoomed in so close that the entire ballroom can see our pores up on the massive screen on stage.

"I am smiling."

"Smile wider." I squeeze Noel's thigh, which only makes his scowl deeper.

We're both nervous. I keep telling myself that this isn't a big deal. It doesn't matter if we win. Our subscription numbers are up and our videos are doing great. We don't need this win to validate all the work we've done in this past year, but goddamn it, we want to win. We want that external validation. We're both way too competitive to graciously step aside for someone else to take what we deserve.

No wonder we ended up in a years-long rivalry. Now that I think about it, even if Noel had won that first time we were nominated in the same category, I might've been just as petty as he was and we still would've become enemies.

It was inevitable. *We* were inevitable.

"The nominees for this year's Best Flip Fuck video are…"

To read the rest of the bonus scene, sign up for Linden Bell's Very Important Reader newsletter here: bit.ly/ bellamybonus.

## ANGEL

Do you like cinnamon rolls, size differences, and straight guys who aren't so straight? Rhys teaches Angel how to go gay for pay in the next The Camboy Network book, *Angel*, bit.ly/angelbm.

# THANK YOU

If you've enjoyed *Bellamy*, please consider recommending it to your friends. Leave a review on social media, your own blog, Amazon, Goodreads, or Bookbub so other MM romance lovers can get to know Bellamy and Noel too.

If you would like to stay up to date on future Linden Bell books, join the Very Important Reader mailing list here: bit.ly/VIRBellamy.

You can also follow me on:
Instagram - instagram.com/authorlindenbell
Facebook - facebook.com/authorlindenbell
Amazon - amazon.com/author/lindenbell
Goodreads - goodreads.com/authorlindenbell
Bookbub - bookbub.com/authors/linden-bell

# ABOUT LINDEN BELL

Linden Bell writes romances that heat you up and make you smile. Her books are low angst, feel good reads with no third act breakup!

instagram.com/authorlindenbell
facebook.com/authorlindenbell
amazon.com/author/lindenbell
goodreads.com/authorlindenbell
bookbub.com/authors/linden-bell

# ALSO BY LINDEN BELL

Mars Fitness Series

Where the jocks of Mars Fitness meet the nerds of their dreams.

The Camboy Network Series

When sex on camera turns into love behind the scenes.